ONLY
THE
RAIN

OTHER TITLES BY RANDALL SILVIS

ONLY THE RAIN

RANDALL SILVIS

THOMAS & MERCER

Published by Thomas & Mercer, Seattle

www.apub.com

Amazon, the Amazon logo, and Thomas & Mercer are trademarks of Amazon.com, Inc., or its affiliates.

ISBN-13: 9781542049948 (hardcover)
ISBN-10: 1542049946 (hardcover)
ISBN-13: 9781542045742 (paperback)
ISBN-10: 1542045746 (paperback)

Cover design by Shasti O'Leary Soudant

Printed in the United States of America

First Edition

This book is for my sons,
Bret and Nathan,
heart of my soul, soul of my heart.

Hey Spence.

It's been a long time, brother. Not that I haven't thought about you since leaving you back there in the sandbox with the camel spiders and sand vipers. A couple days ago I read an article that said Iraq is the most dangerous place in the world, and not just because of its animals. I guess we can attest to that, huh?

Those days are never far from my thoughts, which means you aren't either. Doing what we did over there, living the way we lived, it's always going to be a part of me, like it or not.

More and more lately, as a matter of fact. For a long time now I've been waking up in the middle of the night, seems like it's always between 0200 and 0300, and I'll go sit at the kitchen table or on the couch in front of the TV, and I'll be telling myself I ought to sit down at the computer and send you an e-mail like I used to. Stupid, huh? An exercise in futility, as you used to say.

Thing is, there's just too much I have to tell somebody, and nobody else I can tell it to. So here I am at the computer tonight instead of staring at the TV or the back of my eyelids. 0249. I'm finally doing it. Cindy and the girls are sleeping like the angels they are, the house is quiet as a tomb, and it feels good to think we're maybe connecting up again.

Question is, where to start. Cause it's hard jumping right into the story, you know? Just coming right out with it, saying I met this woman and I did this, I did that, and it was maybe the stupidest thing I've ever done, and now I'm terrified about what's going to happen next.

Back in the sandbox I would have walked up to you and said, "Can I talk to you a minute, Spence?" and gotten straight to the point. But we were together every day back then, living the same life. Never knew if we'd see another morning or not. I think I'm still pretty much the same guy I was over there, but the details are different. Different routines, different obligations, different people to answer to. Context, you know? That's what you always used to say. Context is everything.

For one thing, I was just a kid over there. Over here I have a pregnant wife and two of the sweetest little girls anybody could imagine. The third one's still an unknown, so new to us that Cindy's old jeans still fit, though she has to keep the top unsnapped now, and only wears them when she goes into town for something other than work. Around the house she mostly wears sweatpants with an elastic top. Even so, another baby on the way has to be factored into all of our plans. I'm the guy responsible for everybody.

Anyway, I guess I'll start by telling you about tonight's dream. I've had it a couple times before, and I wish like hell it would stop. I have this thing that happened to me here, and not very long ago. But somehow in my head it's getting all messed up now with that night we got grabbed out of the rack and had to collect those three bodies in an alleyway, you remember? Three guys laying there in pieces with their rifles stacked in a corner. The one guy was in so many pieces it was hard to tell which parts were his and which belonged to that girl he'd been on top of. And how we were told to leave her where she was, not to bother with her, like we weren't even supposed to see her or know what had been going on there before they all bought the farm.

When I dream about that, I dream it's me on top of her when the IED goes off. In the dream I hear the bag or whatever it was being thrown into the alley and hitting the dirt, and then the boom and all the air gets sucked out of me, and right away I know what it is and that I'm dead as shit, and I have these few moments before waking up when I'm pissed as hell at the people who would do something like that. I mean killing us soldiers is one thing, but what kind of people wouldn't come to help a girl being raped but would sacrifice her like that just to kill some Americans? And I wake up feeling so helpless and guilty and I don't know what all.

Jesus, it was fucked over there, wasn't it?

Anyway, the girl in the dream. It isn't that haji girl I see with me on top of her, both of us about to be blown to pieces, but this other girl I met over here a little while back. To say *met* isn't quite right though, because I didn't even get her name until a week or more later, and by then I wanted to forget all about her and the stupid thing I did. You're probably thinking sex, right? But no, it was way more stupid than that. And way more dangerous.

Thing is, that's all still playing out. It's like I'm waiting for the other shoe to fall. It might be a slipper, or it might be an IED. Worst part is, I can't tell Cindy or the girls or anybody else about it, which is why I'm sitting here at the computer at three in the morning. I asked myself who can I tell and still keep the whole thing a secret, and it was either you or God. I figure God already knows, and that's probably why I can't shake this need to try to get myself clean again.

I just don't know how to get into it without taking you back to what all led up to it. But then I think, am I just trying to rationalize what I did? Blame the circumstances instead of taking the blame like a man? I often wonder about those three soldiers. If they had been caught and arrested and not scooped up into body bags, would they have tried to weasel out of it somehow, or would they have manned up and said, "I did it. I'm guilty as hell"?

Because I feel like I need to say that, Spence. I did it. I'm guilty as hell. And now I can't seem to get over this feeling that I—

Gotta go, Spence. Emma's crying, having a bad dream, I guess, just like her old man. Next time.

*

You remember those times I talked about Pops and Gee, the grandparents who raised me after my mother died? Well, Gee passed a little over a year ago. Pops shuffled around on his own for several months after that, but sank lower and lower, it seemed to me, until one day I took him to check out this independent living place called Brookside Country Manor about six miles from Cindy's and my new house. It took another four months before he surprised me by admitting he'd been visiting it from time to time ever since.

"I booked myself a room in that no-tell motel you took me to," he said.

"What do you mean you booked yourself a room?"

"Plus I lined up a real estate agent to sell the house for me. And one of those storage units for all this junk we accumulated over the years. I could use some help moving it out there one of these days."

So the day before we checked him into his new apartment, I loaded four cardboard boxes of his stuff, all that was left of his life, into the back of my pickup truck, and we drove them out to the edge of town to one of those storage unit places where you can rent a big metal box for fifty dollars a month, one with a concrete floor, and pack away all the things you can't bear to let go of but will probably never hold or look at ever again. We also took a load of old furniture Gee had inherited from her mother, a piece called a secretary and a rolltop desk and a vanity with an hourglass-shaped mirror. Plus a set of four wooden chairs, three of which weren't safe to sit on anymore.

"She must've made me promise at least a dozen times not to sell any of it after she was gone," he said. "I think she thought I was going to make a fortune from it and run off with some showgirl."

4

"In other words, I have to hold onto it forever?"

"Keep it till after I'm in the ground. She'll know by then I couldn't find any showgirls to take me on." And then he grinned those still beautiful white teeth of his. "'Course, I'm not dead yet, so I'm still looking."

I'm sure I must have told you that Pops had been a boxer and a career Marine, retired as an E-7 not long after Hamburger Hill, so one whole box of stuff was left over from those days, maybe thirty pounds of photos and awards, his dress blues with the gold-on-red chevrons on the sleeves, the old brown leather shoes he used to wear in the ring, Gee's big old leather-bound Bible with the family tree she had sketched in on a blank flyleaf, a half-filled scrapbook with shots of him and his buddies, an empty Whitman's Sampler box, the little one that only holds four pieces, and inside it a braid Gee made of her and Pops' hair when they were both young, his jet-black then and hers chestnut brown.

He also had two gun bags, one holding the .30-06 he'd bought for me when I was twelve, and another for his own .30-30. Thing is, I came back from Iraq with absolutely no appetite for hunting again. I told him I'd still go out walking in the woods with him anytime he wanted, but I didn't feel much like killing anything anymore. To my surprise Pops was fine with that. He said the only reason he'd kept it up was cause I seemed to like it.

He said, "I'm guessing you won't be raising those little girls to be hunters either."

"The third one might be a boy though."

"Then hang onto them for a while. Pack them away with everything else. But boy or no boy, my feelings won't be hurt if you'd rather get rid of them. Go ahead and sell them if you can get a good price."

Another box held what Pops called his miscellaneous. He already had it packed and taped shut when I got to his place, and as I was sliding it onto the dolly to wheel it out to my pickup he told me, "This is the one you'll want to open first when I'm gone. It's got all the legal stuff in it. Birth certificates, my will, that cheap gold watch they gave me from the plant, plus a bag of wheatie pennies and old dimes and silver dollars."

"Feels like a lot more than that in here," I told him.

"There's more," he said. "It's stuff I want you to have. I'll keep the key to the storage unit on my keychain, so that's the first thing you'll want to grab."

Ever since he'd made his plans to move to Brookside he'd been talking like he was at death's door. Fact is he was still making up to twenty circuits around the high school track every morning, walking faster than most of the other people there could jog, but he'd had his annual checkup a few months earlier and the quack doctor watched him walk across the room and announced that Pops had Parkinson's disease. I asked how that diagnosis had been reached and Pops said, "It was the way I had my elbows cocked. Classic sign, he said."

I asked, "How the hell are you supposed to walk? With your hands shoved down in your pockets?"

Personally I think Pops was looking for a reason to give up. As likely as he was to still crack a joke, most of the starch went out of him when Gee started to fade. Three strokes in a little over four months, bam, bam, and then bang, the lid slammed shut. I think a big part of Pops got buried with her. I tried to get him to move in with Cindy and me and the girls but he wouldn't do it. He said, "There's not enough room in that place of yours for a man to fart comfortably. A man my age needs his own bathroom."

He didn't want to be a burden to anybody, that's all. He'd rather die alone than let anybody have to take care of him. I didn't understand that kind of reasoning at the time, but I understand it all too well now.

Anyway, the last box we carted off to the storage unit was filled with what he always referred to as "your mother's stuff," meaning the scrapbooks and photos she collected over the years, her few pieces of inexpensive jewelry and a shoebox full of the valentines and drawings and poems I made for her up until I was maybe eleven or twelve and started to believe only sissies do that kind of stuff, plus a couple of quilts she'd made and three afghans she knitted after her back injury left her more or less unable to walk on her own. Pops said I could take those quilts and afghans if I wanted them, put them to good use, he said, the way I did with his and Gee's bedroom suite. He kept two afghans for himself, put the one Gee made on his bed at Brookside and the one from my mom on his recliner, and I think he was a little offended when I didn't take the rest of them.

So as not to hurt his feelings I told him I'd get that box of blankets someday, maybe in the fall when the weather turned cold. Truth is, Cindy didn't want them; she prefers the thick, fluffy comforters and fleece blankets from the department store, said those old quilts and afghans make her think of the Amish, or like something you'd find in an old folks' home or a flea market. It was hard enough to get her to take the bedroom suite, but we were going to need Emma's twin bed for the new baby in a year or so, and we were watching every penny.

I know this makes Cindy sound like a not very nice person, but in fact the opposite is true. We'd got our own place a few months earlier, a three-bedroom ranch in a little development a couple miles out of town, which we were able to buy thanks to the money Pops gave us for the down payment, and Cindy wanted it to be exactly that, our place, not like the HUD double-wide she grew up in, stuffed with hand-me-downs and pillows and knickknacks her mother bought at the Goodwill store.

"Nothing was ever my own," is how Cindy described it. "Clothes, shoes, toys, whatever. They were always somebody else's first. The only reason I ended up with anything was because the other person didn't want it anymore."

That was something Cindy and me shared, I guess, the feeling that we were sort of like somebody else's castoffs. I never had a father other than Pops, and though Cindy had a father she often wished she didn't. Her mother always came over for Christmas and Thanksgiving, even when all we had was that cramped little one-bedroom and only a card table in the kitchen. And Cindy always took her out to get her hair done on her mother's birthday, but as far as I know Cindy never once invited her father anywhere or even asked how he was doing. Up till the trouble started I'd only ever seen him twice myself, and that was enough for me too, I guess. I wish it had stayed that way.

Anyway, none of this really has anything to do with the rest of the story. Or maybe it has everything to do with it, depending on which theory of life you subscribe to. Personally, I've come to believe that theories are of small value when it comes to actually living your life, to making all the hard decisions you have to make and then dealing with the consequences of those decisions.

And there are always consequences, that's the one truth I know for sure. That's something you kept telling us, Spence, remember? And reminding us that sometimes the good consequences are as hard to swallow as the bad.

"You just do it," is how Pops would put it. "You do it and then you live with it."

Okay, that's enough for tonight. I got to work in the morning, same as always. Better catch a little shut-eye if I can. Talk to you again soon. I promise to get to the point next time.

*

The thing I remember about that day all the trouble started was looking out the kitchen window and wondering if I was going to get wet riding my motorcycle to work that morning. Cindy was always good at knowing what I was thinking, and she said, "You want me to get the girls up?"

It wasn't quite 6:30 yet, which meant dragging the girls out of bed a good hour earlier than usual so she could give me a ride to work. Then she'd have to rush back home, get Dani and Emma fed and dressed for daycare and get herself ready for her teller job at the bank. We'd done it before but I always felt bad asking her to do it. Back when I finally got my job at the rock-crushing plant and we were able to get this house, our plan had been to pick up a secondhand compact for Cindy as soon as we could put a few dollars aside. But then Pops got another ticket for driving too slow, and he said we could probably have his Lumina next June because that was when his license came up for renewal and the odds were ten to one against it being renewed. So that was when Cindy decided that instead of buying a car she wanted us to try for a boy one more time, and after that I would get a vasectomy. It was important to both of us that all our kids were planned and in every way intentional. We both agreed there are already too many people on the planet, and though we understand the math behind zero population growth, it also seemed that since we were both only children, with three grandparents and one mother already gone, and two fathers more or less missing in action, then we maybe deserved a little wiggle room for a third child.

So Cindy read a book about the various tricks we could try in order to increase the chances of having a boy, things like using lemon juice to change the pH of Cindy's body and so forth. The thing that made the most sense to us was when she read that the boy sperms are faster swimmers than the girl sperms, but the boys die off sooner. The girls are slower swimmers but they have more stamina. So the thing to do was to get the boys as close to their target as possible before they all tired out and died.

We used the position illustrated in the book, and afterward Cindy laid on the floor for an hour with her legs up on the bed and a fat pillow under her butt. All this was supposed to give the boy swimmers a downhill swim, I guess. We did that two nights in a row and then the next morning Cindy said, "Well, it took. I'm pregnant." I said she couldn't possibly know that already and she said, "Trust me. I know." She was so sure of herself she wouldn't even let me buy her a pregnancy kit at Walmart. "Waste of money," she said. "I know what I know. I know I'm pregnant and I know it's a boy."

There's no use arguing with a woman when her mind's made up, so I just quit trying. Besides, she's spooky like that sometimes. Seems to know stuff she has no way of knowing. Which only makes matters more worrisome for me since I got into this trouble I'm going to tell you about.

Anyway, it wasn't two weeks later she was puking before breakfast. So I guess she did know what she was talking about. Whether the book did or not remains to be seen.

The reason I'm telling you all this is so you'll understand what our situation was when the trouble started. Despite the inconvenience of not having a second car, the situation was full of hope. We were still living paycheck to paycheck but life was really starting to look good for us, and not in a pie-in-the-sky kind of way either. We even picked out a name for our new boy: David Russell. He had Pops' first name and my name for his middle name. We still didn't know for sure that he'd be a boy but I decided to think positive and maybe all our good thoughts would work the necessary magic.

I had a new job and a new vasectomy scar, and Cindy and Dani and Emma and Maybe-Davy and me all had a new house to live in. It wasn't a cast-off house either. It wasn't a hand-me-down. It was brand-new construction, three bedrooms and two bathrooms. It's only sixteen hundred square feet on a quarter-acre lot in a small development of twelve homes lined up along both sides of a cul-de-sac. I wasn't crazy about having a house that was exactly like eleven other families' but Cindy loves it. "It makes me feel normal for a change," she said. "Like we're all in the same boat together."

And then one gray morning my whole world went upside down. If I had let Cindy drive me to work that day instead of riding the motorcycle, it never would've happened. Gee always used to say, "God works in mysterious ways." But as much as I loved her and appreciate all the things she did for me, I think maybe my former staff sergeant might have understood life better than she did.

"If you even once happen to look the wrong way," you used to tell us, "if you so much as fucking blink out here, you're gonna find yourself getting raped by an elephant."

And that's exactly what happened to me that day, Spence. I looked the wrong fucking way.

*

I mentioned my motorcycle last time and now this thought keeps interrupting my other thoughts, if you know what I mean. I can't ever climb onto my bike, or usually even pass it in the garage, without remembering that medic on my, what was it, second or third day in-country. The one who was riding around the FOB on his Honda and got his leg blown off during an attack. There we all were crowding around the medevac bird telling him he was going to be okay, and him pleading and pleading for some drugs to knock him out.

I was embarrassed to admit I didn't even know the dude's name yet, so I wasn't going to ask anybody about it, but I've never been able to get him out of my head, not even back here at home. So one day when I was out riding by myself I decided I'd come up with a name for him, and I started running through the alphabet, thinking up every name I could, until I came to one that felt like it fit him. I remember he was sort of thin and had sandy blond hair, and I also remember his eyes being a pale blue that most girls would kill for. And the name I gave him finally was Springer. Don't ask me why, but when I heard it inside my head I thought, that's it, he's Springer.

I dream about him sometimes. I dream about the two of us riding up north into the big forests up there, cruising along in and out of the sunlight and shadows, riding parallel to the river with the sunlight shimmering like silver leaves in the ripples and rapids. He's got both legs in those dreams, and he's always got the biggest fucking grin on his face. And his name's always Springer. I mean without a doubt, I never even question it, he's always Springer in those dreams.

And we're riding along side by side on our bikes, not a care in the world. Except that I'm watching him and thinking, the poor sonofa-bitch doesn't have clue one about what's going to happen to him.

Is that a weird dream to be having or what?

*

Sorry about how short my last e-mail was. Sometimes I get all, you know, emotional when I'm remembering stuff. When that happens I have to just lean away from the keyboard and get my shit together again. Don't want to rain on the electronics, you know what I mean?

Anyway, I'll go back to telling you about that morning the real story here actually started, and me riding the bike into work as usual even though a thunderstorm was in the forecast. My boss waited till after lunch that day to call me into the office. For some reason, the moment I heard my name coming through the loudspeaker, I knew it was the voice of doom calling. Truth is I'd felt funny all day, even before I'd left the house. There was a weird heaviness in my chest that morning, like I couldn't get enough air into my lungs because they were already filled up with something else, with some kind of gray fog maybe that had settled into me during the night. But when I got to the plant that morning without being hit by a single drop of rain, I chalked the feeling up to nervousness about the weather, and told myself it was the air that was heavy, all that damp August air I'd sucked in because Cindy liked to sleep with the windows open.

Thinking back on it now, the only other time I had that feeling in my chest was in Mahmudiya. I remember waking up with that feeling for most of a week, and how all throughout the day I felt like I was pushing through water, like the sand under my feet was the ocean floor. This was in the second week of February—you know where I'm going with this? The city was full of Shia Muslims for that festival they call Arbaeen. I remember how strange it was to see people crawling through the streets on their hands and knees, all to show their allegiance to Muhammad's grandson. But it was also damn impressive they could have so much respect for a guy who got beheaded a thousand years or so ago. The only thing people in this country might crawl through the streets for is a chance to win a big-screen TV.

Anyway, you kept reminding us to expect some kind of trouble, what with those millions of Shias in the city. "It's supposed to be a really peaceful time for the Shias," you told us, "but you can expect the Sunnis to see it as a prime opportunity to fuck up somebody's day."

Our squad was on security detail along the road leading up to the grandson's shrine, just standing there watching and making our presence known. When the propane tank exploded it made this *woo-whooom* kind of sound, first the bomb itself and then, before you could even think, bomb!, the tank explosion. I felt the air punch into my ears and smack me in the face and then I went down hard on my ass. I never even noticed that shard of metal stuck in my interceptor vest until you pointed it out to me. Funny thing is, after you checked under my vest, then pulled out the hunk of metal and handed it to me and I saw there was no blood on it, my chest didn't feel heavy anymore. That heavy fog feeling I'd had all week was gone. Except that now there were dozens of other people dead and dying, bleeding and crying and screaming, when all they'd wanted was to be peaceful and pray.

In any case, the heaviness I had that morning at the plant was like the first heaviness in Mahmudiya, not like the other one I get whenever I think about those dead pilgrims, or about Springer or Pops and my mother and Gee. I was doing my usual rounds, making sure every-body was busy, when out of nowhere my boss Jake's amplified voice cut through the cloud of limestone dust like a kind of muffled explosion, but I felt its punch all the same. "Attention, Russell. Attention Russell Blystone. Please stop by the office before you clock out. Thank you."

Thing is, there was absolutely no reason for that announcement. At the end of the day I always change clothes and shower off the worst of the dust, and then I have to walk right past Jake's door on my way to the bike, which I keep parked up against the rear of his building so it stays relatively clear of the dust. Most of what we produced was a fine aggregate used for highway construction and concrete reinforcement, but that week we were filling an order for talcum that was headed to Indonesia. So that week was a particularly dusty one for me, what with the slightest breeze stirring up the material on the conveyer belts as well as in the big piles.

But whatever kind of order we were filling, it was always my routine to say "See you tomorrow" or "See you Monday" to Jake on my way out, unless it was the second or fourth Friday of the month, in which case he'd be sitting there with my pay envelope in his hand. So for him to make that announcement over the loudspeaker when it was completely unnecessary, well, I couldn't do anything but stand there in that thick cloud of talcum and feel like every last drop of air had been sucked right out of me. I think I even took off my mask, which is a stupid thing to do when you're enveloped in white dust. All I remember for sure is staggering over to the office building while coughing my lungs out. Even now I can taste that dust in my mouth. It's a gritty, chalky, suffocating memory I'm not likely to forget.

"Stop right there," Jake said when I stepped into his doorway. "I said before you clock out. Not this very minute. Meaning after you've showered and changed clothes first."

"I'm here now," I told him. "What's up?"

"You must've left a trail of dust the whole way down the hallway."

"Did something happen to Cindy or one of the girls?"

"Nothing like that," he said. "Come back in an hour when you're supposed to."

"Tell me now. I'm already here."

"You look like Casper the fucking ghost," he said. "You're not stepping in here looking like that. And I don't want to have to tell you this without us sitting down face to face."

"Are you firing me?" I said. I couldn't believe he ever would, being a friend of Pops and all, and having told Pops several times already how glad he was to have me there. He'd said that in almost forty years I was the only foreman who ever went voluntarily down to the pulverizer to check on things. The only one who'd scramble up a belt if he had to, or get his hands up inside a piece of jammed equipment. Plus he was always joking around with me when I was at my desk across from him, working on my reports. Out of the blue he might ask me something like, "Anybody ever tell you you look a lot like Billy Conn?"

And I might answer back something like, "You mean James Caan, the actor? The guy from *Honeymoon in Vegas*? Man, he's a dinosaur. He's almost as old as you."

To which he would say his standard line, "You fucking college kids, that's all you know about, isn't it? Movies and television and all that Internet stuff."

I know all about Billy Conn, of course. You can't have a grandfather who was a boxer and not know about "The Pittsburgh Kid." I could even have quoted that line from *On the Waterfront*, which was Pops' favorite movie of all time. And I don't mean Marlon Brando's line, the one everybody knows, when Brando says, "I could've been a contender." I mean the one Rod Steiger says, "You could've been another Billy Conn."

So not only did Jake like me but I was the best foreman he'd ever had. Plus he knew I was a veteran, and that fact cut a lot of ice as far as he was concerned. Plus I was his friend's grandson. So he never would have fired me unless maybe I'd seduced his wife and their daughter and their granddaughter and then ate the Limburger cheese and onion sandwich he had every day for lunch.

"I told you a couple weeks ago that the Chinese made me an offer on the plant," he said.

"And you also told me you probably wouldn't sell. And if you did, it wouldn't affect my job anyway. You said they'd need to keep me and at least a couple of the other guys on."

"I was hoping," he said. "But they say otherwise. Said they're bringing in all their own people. In fact they're selling all the equipment off for scrap, turning this into a high-tech operation. Bringing the whole shebang over prefabricated from China."

I felt like I wanted to throw up. But it wouldn't have done me any good to argue with him. The deal was done, I could see it in his eyes.

"How long do I have?"

"Shutdown on September 1."

"Ten days?" I said. "We have orders to fill."

"Canceled," he said. "Russell, I'm sorry. You have no fucking idea how sorry I am."

"I've barely been here half a year."

"I know. And I know what I said when I hired you. Put in a year as the foreman, then I'd bring you in to handle all the accounts. Put in five more years to prove you could run this place, and I'd give you a chance to buy me out."

"Except that you didn't know about the Chinese then."

"The only thing I knew about the Chinese is . . . Well, hell. Fuck what I thought I knew and didn't. You'll find another job soon enough. And until you do you can sit at home and collect unemployment."

"I'm not eligible for unemployment," I told him.

"The hell you're not."

I told him I collected that whole time I was home and without a job after my discharge. Used up all my eligibility. Then three and a half years on the GI Bill getting my business degree. "I started here the day after graduation," I said. "I haven't worked long enough to collect unemployment again."

"Then welfare for a few months. I mean fuck it, Russell. You'll do whatever you have to do. You have a family to think about."

But by then I felt like my chest was being crushed. Cindy has a job at the bank, so there was no way I'd be able to get welfare. No way I'd even think about it even if I could.

I told Jake all that, and he said, "Well you better at least check it out. Fuck your pride. You know where my pride is right now? And I'm not even talking about all the ways the EPA's been squeezing my balls for the past forty years. Charlie Chan said if I didn't sell, they'd fill in the quarry and put their plant there, undercut all my prices, steal all my customers. I'd be bankrupt by the end of the year. That was the deal I was offered."

All I could do was to stand there in Jake's doorway and shake my head. It wasn't going to do any good to plead or beg or cry, no matter how much I wanted to. I couldn't breathe, couldn't think, couldn't even see the whole room for a while, like my peripheral vision had shut down. I started falling to the side and caught myself against the doorframe.

Jake came up out of his chair. "You okay?" he said.

I held up my hand and nodded, though I wasn't okay at all.

"You need a drink of water or something?"

"I need a job, Jake."

He settled back into his chair, and neither of us said anything for a while.

Once I felt like I could move without falling down, I turned to leave.

"One last thing," he said. "I need you and the other fellas to keep this under your hat for a while. I know you got to tell your wives but don't be spreading it all over town just yet. The new owners think there might be protests or something once the word gets out."

"There ought to be protests," I said.

He didn't like hearing that. "It's business, Russell. Don't be pretending you wouldn't do the same fucking thing if you was in my position."

I didn't want to get into it with him. It wouldn't have done any good. Besides, I needed to get some air into my lungs. I needed to get outside and find a private place to sit down for a couple minutes. So that's what I did.

I know how Gee would have handled that situation. She would have sighed and stopped knitting for a minute or two. Then she would have said, not to me or anybody else but more to herself, and not with any measure of happiness as you might expect from someone counting on an eternity in Paradise, but more like a kind of moan with words added to it, "The Lord giveth and the Lord taketh away."

And for some reason these days, every time I think of what Gee might say in a certain situation, I also think what you might say, Spence. I swear to God I can hear the words coming right out of your mouth. "Life's a shit pie, soldier. But when that's all you're given to eat, you better learn to like the taste of it."

*

The thing that sometimes has me thinking our lives might really be controlled by the stars and planets and birthdates and such, or else by malicious gods or spirits, or by anything other than coincidence and chance, and sure as hell not by a god that wishes us well, is the fact that bad things never happen one at a time. And when they do happen, they seem to pick the very worst minute for it.

Take the rain, for example. Even before I left the house that morning, I'd been expecting one of those August cloudbursts that starts with a thunderclap and then keeps on hammering down until there are little rivers and lakes running through the streets and yards. If the rain had hit in the morning, it would have been an inconvenience but not much more. If it had hit during working hours, the rain would have tamed the ferocious heat and kept the dust down. But of course neither of those things happened.

The first thunderclap shook the tiles while I was standing there in the shower, with the cool spray pelting my head while I leaned against the wall and wondered what the hell I was going to do for a job. I knew I had to start looking immediately. In ten days I would be without an income. Cindy was only bringing home a little over a thousand a month, and our mortgage alone would eat up most of that.

In my head I started running through all of our other expenses, and with each one my legs got a little bit weaker, and my chest hurt a little bit more. Pretty soon the water hitting my head and shoulders felt like a thousand little fists pounding me down. There were the utilities, meaning cable and Internet and sewage and water and electricity and gas. Plus insurance on my truck and bike and on the house. The real estate and school taxes. A family of four to feed with a baby on the way. Dani would be starting first grade after Labor Day and needed clothes and school supplies. And Jesus, health insurance. I was carrying everybody on my policy because the one Cindy had at the bank was virtually worthless. How the hell were we going to pay for all that?

In the blink of an eye we'd gone from being secure and hopeful to being one step from homeless. Except that I was the only one who knew it.

And oh yeah, the rain. By the time I dried off and dressed, the rain was coming down in buckets. The gravel parking lot looked like a steaming island about to go under. I had my rain gear in the saddlebags, but by the time I got the cover off the bike I was already soaked to the skin, plus so weak with fear that I figured, what good is rain gear? So I jammed my helmet on and swung my leg over the wet seat and fired up the engine.

Then as I'm pulling around the corner of the building, there's Jake standing outside his door, holding a magazine over his head against the downpour, and yelling at me to put the bike in his truck, he'd give me a ride home. I just kept on going. The sky was black as pitch except for the occasional lightning. Even my high beam had to struggle to make a difference. The long gravel lane down to the highway already had two little rivers gushing down the ruts the trucks had made, so I was forced to ride the hump down the middle in first gear, tapping the hand and foot brakes all the way and dragging my feet for balance.

The highway wasn't much better. Two-wheeled vehicles have a tendency to slide on wet pavement. When that wet pavement is also coated with a fine layer of grit from a thousand little streams of runoff, the highway can be deadly for a biker. So, whether I wanted to go slow or not, I was forced to cut my speed to half what it would have been on a dry day. It was cut by half again by the nervous nellies in their cars. Once I hit town, traffic was moving at a crawl. And then it came to a complete halt. I was stopped dead in a downpour, still a mile and a half from the blacktop road that would take me the last few miles home. I just wanted to lay down in the ditch and cry.

I considered riding the shoulder up to my turnoff, but wanted to see what was causing the traffic snarl. If it was something I could drive around, I'd give it a try. So I shut the bike off and parked it right where it sat, then started walking up the side of the road. It wasn't long before I saw the red and blue lights up ahead, two squad cars parked one behind the other on the shoulder. That was when I also saw the tow truck in the other lane, blocking the oncoming traffic as the driver tried to maneuver close enough to get a hook on an SUV broadside on the road. The SUV driver had apparently attempted a U-turn only to be slammed into by oncoming traffic. I couldn't make out the kind of vehicle that T-boned the SUV, but I could see a cop with a flashlight waving my lane of traffic back, trying to make room for the tow truck.

By now I'm maybe twenty feet from my bike, and the cars in front of it are slowly inching backward. I turned and sprinted back to my bike and got there just in time to pound a fist on the trunk of the car in front of me. I caught him maybe two seconds from running over the bike—an accident that, in the long run, would have produced a better outcome than the one that lay ahead.

I hopped on the bike and got it turned around, and then I back-tracked to where there was a one-lane blacktop I thought would prob-ably get me close to home again. I'd been down that particular road only once I could remember, one of those Sundays in spring when the world seems a wide-open place full of warmth and sunshine. Cindy and the girls were at a birthday party that day, so I was using my free time to take the bike out on a shakedown cruise.

One of the things I liked to do best back then was to find an unfa-miliar road and explore it, just to see where it might take me. I would turn this way or that, taking any stretch of blacktop that promised new scenery. And somehow I made it onto SR218, a narrow piece of road flanked mostly by fields or hardwood forests, full of tight turns and a couple long straightaways. That was all I remembered about the road, except that it ran basically north to south and joined up with Route 62 at the Get-Go station. Route 62 junctioned with Route 7, my usual road home.

I wasn't on 218 more than a few minutes before the rain let up to a drizzle. I was able to loosen my death grip on the handlebars, and some of the tightness in my back and shoulders lightened up too. I was still getting drenched, not that any more rain could get me wetter than I already was. Still, I started breathing a little bit easier. A ride on the bike always does that for me once I get away from the traffic. And I couldn't have been more alone on that back road. Plus, still having to keep my speed down to forty or so, I could smell the wet fields and trees now. The fields were thick with either corn or soybeans, two shades of green both darkened by the gray sky, but the air was sweet and cool, and even the water shining on the blacktop made it all look cleaner.

And then I passed the house off to my right at the bottom of a low hill. I saw the girl from maybe fifty yards away. She was dancing in the yard and she was as naked as the day she was born. At first I assumed she was a little kid, but that impression didn't last. She was a long way from being a kid, in her midtwenties probably, maybe even closer than that to my own age. And I will admit that the moment I saw her I started slowing down. A fine young girl dancing naked in the rain is not something you're likely to see every day.

This one was making slow turns with her arms held out at her sides. Sometimes she'd be looking up at the sky, sometimes down at the muddy ground, weaving and swaying. It kind of reminded me of some scene from a movie, like a pagan rain dance, you know? In the background the thunder was still rumbling now and then, but getting farther and farther away from us.

Between the rumbles I could catch bits of what must have been very loud music coming from inside the house, which was a run-down kind of place with a couple of blue plastic chairs on the front porch, another chair holding open the door. I can still hear that music in my head, though I didn't hear it clearly that day until I shut off the bike. But every time I hear it these days I can still picture her dancing, still see her long mud-splattered legs, her small breasts and the hair that I thought then was brown. I saw her afterward, in drier times, and that was when I realized her hair was strawberry blonde. It was the rain that made it look darker. So now every time I hear Gregg Allman singing "Someday Baby," whether I hear it on the radio or in one of the dreams I sometimes have, I see her and I see the brindled pit bull pulling at his chain, barking and wagging his tail like he's going crazy wanting to dance with her. But she always keeps a step or two beyond the reach of his chain, which is looped around a big black oak to the side of the house.

So I go riding past her house as slow as I can without coming to a stop. If she sees me, she gives no sign of it. I'm still taking quick looks back at her even after I pass the house. And that's when I see her go down in the mud. I see one bare foot slip out from under her, go up in the air, and then she goes down hard on her back.

I come to a stop as fast as I can on the slippery road, turn around on my seat and wait for her to get up. But she isn't moving. The dog is straining at his chain harder than ever and barking like he's possessed. I keep waiting and waiting, because the one thing I do not want to do is to be caught leaning over a naked woman who is not my wife. Make that two things: I also do not want my throat ripped out by a pit bull.

But in the end I have no choice. I sit there watching for what seems at least a couple of minutes but is probably less. She's as motionless as a doll laying there in the mud. I can't just ride away and leave her there.

"This is where a guy gets himself into trouble," you said one time. "Helping somebody that don't want help."

You were saying it to that guy Keith who nearly got himself—

Gotta go. I hear Cindy in the bathroom.

*

Sorry about bailing last night, brother. Turns out Cindy had too much iced tea before going to bed. But I made it back under the sheet before she even knew I'd been gone. Not that it would have been a big deal or anything; she's used to waking up and finding my half of the bed empty. But she worries when that happens, you know? Always wants to talk it out. Which is the last thing I want to do with a civilian. Wouldn't do either of us any good.

So back to what I was saying last night about helping somebody who don't want help. I remember you warning that big goofy guy from Ohio named Keith. He was standing there shaking like a leaf beside an Al Jubouri woman on her hands and knees screaming over the body of a guy who turned out to be her husband. Before this our platoon had been standing around the outdoor market that morning, keeping an eye out for anybody looking out of place, the gunners behind their .50 cals in the HMMWVs, same old same old. The woman had been doing her damnedest to raise one of those pull-down metal covers on a shop front, but the thing was stuck and the man with her never once offered to help, just stood there chattering away in Arabic. I could tell by his tone he was criticizing her, maybe even threatening her. That was when Keith broke away and walked over to her and bent down and put his hand on top of hers to help lift the cover.

I remember Keith being one of those guys who's always smiling and nodding, always agreeing with everything you say. But if you looked into his eyes, you could tell he didn't really comprehend most of what was going on. The kind of guy who never should've been in the military in the first place. Should've been on a playground somewhere teaching ten-year-olds how to play checkers and badminton, things like that.

Anyway, the Al Jubouri guy obviously doesn't like his woman being touched, and truth is Keith should have known better in the first place, he had the same training all of us had. But it was what it was, and before you know it the husband pulls this long skinny knife out of his pants and is moving in on Keith. And of course now, at the worst possible moment, Keith's training kicks in and *bambambam* the guy is on the ground, motionless as a stone. Only thing moving is the smoke rising out the barrel of Keith's M4. I remember the smell too, that stench of burned propellant, and how for a few moments it's the only smell in the air, stronger even than the sewage stink. And then all of a sudden the wife's throwing herself down on top of her husband and wailing while he bleeds out on the ground, and the next instant there's people running and screaming and cursing all over the place.

The only thing that saved Keith's skin was that all of us immediately surrounded the scene with weapons at the ready so nobody would come along and attempt to swipe the knife. We got photos of the guy laying there with the knife still in his hand.

After the investigation, when Keith spent the rest of his tour manning a radio back at the FOB, I told myself it was the best place for him. Probably where we all should have been.

I'm guessing incidents like this one kept playing over and over in your head same as they do for me now. That's why you never got tired of preaching at us, every time we'd go out on patrol. "We're here to protect these people, not kill them. Kill one of them, and next day six of their relatives join the insurgency. Next day there's more bombs on the road. Then it's gonna be some of us bleeding out on the ground."

I can't tell you how many times in the past months I've wished you'd been around last summer the day I lost my job. Wish you'd been standing there in that soggy yard when I climbed off my bike. "You turn your ass around, soldier," you would have said. "You get back on your pony and ride."

In some ways, I guess, I have a lot in common with Keith.

Because there I am running over to the naked girl, splashing up muddy water with every step, that pit bull going absolutely foaming-mouth berserk at the sight of me, and me leaning over to ask if she's all right only to see her laying there all spacey-eyed and giggling as if the rain on her face is the funniest thing she's felt in her entire life.

"You okay?" I ask her. "You took a pretty hard fall."

She reaches up and puts her wet hands on the back of my neck and sings along with the music coming out of the house. And stupid me, I can't help but smile at her. Even with that pit bull barking and snarling a few inches from my face, all but spraying me with his saliva, I thought she had a really sweet voice. And what man isn't going to smile when a pretty, naked girl is singing to him with her arms around his neck?

"Listen," I told her. "You need to get inside. You're all goosebumpy. Plus, if somebody else comes along and sees you like this . . . this isn't the smartest thing for you to be doing."

She raised herself up then like she wanted me to kiss her, but then she winced and moaned and tightened up for a second. I said, "Tell me where it hurts. Does it hurt in your back?"

"Mmmm," she said, so I slid one hand under her shoulders and the other to the small of her back, trying to feel if anything was broken. Not that I would have known anyway. They don't teach you that in business administration.

All I really accomplished was to give her a chance to roll over into my arms. That's when she stopped singing and said, "Carriemeehin."

It took me a few seconds to decipher that, what with her slurring her words together. I couldn't smell any alcohol or weed so I figured she was high on coke or ecstasy or something like that. I was just guessing, though, since I've never gone beyond weed myself, and that stopped the day I met Cindy.

"You want me to carry you inside?" I said to the girl, and she said, "Mmm."

I looked up and out across the yard then, because I was thinking what if somebody drives past and sees me carrying her into the house naked? I'd passed only a few houses on the way here and they were Amish places set way back from the road, but I wasn't worried about the Amish. I was worried about somebody calling Cindy and saying, "Russell rides a Road Star, doesn't he? With a blue metal-flake paint job and leather saddlebags and no windshield?"

Truth is I was kind of frozen there in indecision for a while, my hands on her wet skin and my knees in the mud. If that dog hadn't jerked itself an inch closer to me, I might still be in the same position.

So then I'm carrying her up onto the porch and she's hugging up against me and moaning every now and then with her mouth pressed into my neck. I stop outside the open door and call inside a couple of times. "Hello? Anybody in here? Hellooo? Anybody home?"

I get no answer from anybody, not even Gregg Allman. The music has stopped and there's this three-way conversation going on between that crazy dog and the pattering rain and my heart thumping like the wings of a flushed grouse.

I say to her, "If I put you down, can you walk inside?"

Her grip around my neck tightens and she pushes herself up tighter against me. "Um mm," she says. "Doan' pu' mee down."

This whole description I'm giving you is probably coming off a lot funnier than it actually was. Truth is I was scared to death. Either that pit bull was going to rip its chain loose and come flying at me, or some burly boyfriend was going to appear with a shotgun in his hands, or somebody who knew Cindy was going to drive by and think, isn't that Russell there with that naked girl in his arms?

If you'd ever been married, you'd know which option I feared the most. Which is why I went ahead and stepped over the threshold and off to the side of the doorway.

So I'm standing in the living room now, bare plank floors and a ratty old couch and matching chair and a coffee table covered with water rings and cigarette burns and empty beer bottles. The only thing out of place is the sixty-inch plasma TV and surround-sound speakers.

"I don't want to put you down in here," I told her. "You've got mud all over you."

This was where she spoke her first real sentence, the first one I heard clearly anyway, even though she was doing her darnedest to shove a wet hand down inside my pants. "Lemme suck your dick," she said.

I have to admit, that gave me a few moments pause. Then I told her, "Sweetheart, I'm a married man with two and a half kids, and you are high as a kite on who knows what. Tell me where to put you down and I'm outta here."

She giggled a little bit, and then she said, "Bathroom."

I'm thinking, good, she wants to get warm and wash off the mud, so I'll dump her in the tub and be on my way. I carried her down the hall, glancing into the rooms as I passed. I had already seen the kitchen from the living room, and I didn't like what I saw. Compared to the living room it was all too orderly and clean, no dishes in the sink, not a damn thing on the counter or the little table. And by now I've also noticed that every window is covered with black poster paper, the kind I buy at Walmart for Dani to draw on with her colored chalk. And the whole place has a vague ammonia stink to it, like some cat's been pissing in every corner, except that there's no cat to be seen, only that brute of a dog outside with the most evil of intentions.

The other two rooms I pass are almost empty, bare to the walls except for an old mattress and pillow on the floor in each of them. Laying on one of the mattresses is what must be the girl's clothes, a pair of cut-off jeans and a yellow T-shirt. Then finally I get to the bathroom, which has this little claw-footed tub filled with plastic buckets full of rags, plus the toilet and sink and a shower stall covered with a blue plastic curtain. The girl's still holding around my neck with one arm but her right hand is digging around in my pants, and I can't tell if she's breaking out in head-to-toe shivers because she's so horny or freezing to death.

I tell her, "You need to get warm. Tub or shower?"

"Gotta pee-pee," she says.

So I set her on her feet beside the toilet. Her hand slips out of my pants but then she grabs my dick from the outside. She sits there and starts to tinkle, all the time grinning up at me and shivering and squeezing my dick, and yeah, I should've pulled away from her right then. I should've run for my life. But I just stood there for half a minute or so and enjoyed it.

But then I thought of Cindy and the girls and that was all I needed. I pulled away from her and said something about putting her in the shower. Then I yanked open the plastic curtain to the shower stall, and in there's a stack of four cardboard boxes of slightly different sizes. Men's boot boxes stacked up over the drain. All but the top one has duct tape sealing them shut. And I think, shoeboxes in the shower? So I lift the lid off the top box. And the dizziness that hits me when I see all those neat bundles of cash inside is enough to make me stagger.

I'm out of breath suddenly and my knees are wobbly. When she stands up and puts her arms around me it's all I can do to pull both dirty towels off the rack and sort of press them into her hands. I look around for more towels but there aren't any, so I scoop her up again and stumble back to the bedroom where her clothes are, and I kick the clothes out of the way and lay her down on the mattress and tuck the two dirty towels around her.

"You need to get yourself dressed," I tell her. She keeps saying things like, baby I'm cold, baby fuck me, and she's touching herself and trying to touch me and my head is spinning and my ears are buzzing like a band saw. I'm, I don't know . . . stunned, I guess, by what I've stumbled into. And I can't breathe. I'm sucking air but it's not doing me any good. I feel the same way I did when the propane tank exploded in Mahmudiya and the ringing in my ears started and all I saw was people bleeding, and for a few moments I think, I'm back there again, that there's some weird kind of juxtaposition of time going on, and when I take a last look down at that naked, muddy girl, I honestly don't know if it's mud or blood all over the mattress.

I do know that I got out of that room and pulled the door shut behind me. And then I'm back out on the porch again, trying to fill my lungs and my head with something I can understand. There's still a light rain coming down, and the pit bull starts into his barking again the moment he sees me. But there's my bike out there at the end of the yard. The rain is falling and the leaves on the trees in the background are a dark, shiny green. I'm thinking to myself that it must be after five by now and in twenty minutes or so Cindy will be home with the girls. And that brings the whole day back to me then. That brings back all the fear and near panic I'd been feeling on my ride away from the plant.

I turned and went back into the house. Got as far as the hallway, then turned around and went back out onto the porch.

Thinking about that now, me knowing what I should do but not wanting to do it, just standing there sort of paralyzed on the porch, reminds me of the day I left for basic. I was barely eighteen, a month out of high school. Pops and Gee drove me to the bus station. And just before I climbed up onto that bus, after we'd already told each other goodbye a half-dozen times, Gee reaches up and lays both hands on my cheeks and pulls me down close to her. She was just a little woman but so serious sometimes, with this life-or-death look in her eyes that almost made me want to laugh at her. "'Watch and pray,'" she says, quoting from the Bible, "'that you do not fall into temptation.'"

That's from Matthew somewhere. It's when Jesus comes back from praying and finds the disciples all asleep and bitches out Peter for being careless. "The spirit is willing," Jesus tells him, "but the flesh is weak."

He might as well have been saying that to me. I wish he'd shown up and joined me on that porch. Because that was my moment, years and years after Gee warned me. I was weak in both spirit and flesh.

The thing is, I couldn't get myself to go down off those steps, no matter how much I knew that's exactly what I needed to do. I couldn't force myself to go back out into the rain and climb onto the bike and take all my fear and . . . what's the word for it . . . uselessness back to Cindy. Not when I had another option.

"Fuck your pride," Jake had said. "You have a family to think about."

"You just do it," is what Pops used to say. "You do it and then you live with it."

And you, Spence . . . the guy who kept me alive all those months, the guy who got me back home vertical, I could hear you too. I swear I could hear you standing there on that porch and whispering in my ear. "It's all about survival, man. Priority one. Don't you ever forget that, soldier."

So I went back inside. I peeked into the bedroom where the girl was, and she was laying there on her back with her eyes closed, waving her hands in the air and singing, which when I think about it was that same Jackson Brown song you and me used to listen to in the afternoons sometimes when it was too frigging hot to move. I honestly don't know if she was really singing that song or not. Maybe it was only inside my head.

Anyway, I went back to the bathroom. I grabbed one of the taped-up boxes. Then I went out to my bike. I don't know if the girl was still singing or not. I don't know if the dog was barking or if the rain was falling or anything else that happened.

The fog of war, they call it. And I took a long ride home through that blinding fog of war.

*

When I got home that night with the box of money in my saddlebag, I didn't know what to do. My mind was racing with all kinds of thoughts. Cindy had put my garage door up after she pulled the pickup in, so I drove into my stall and parked the bike half-turned toward the door the way I always do. What little of me had dried out inside the naked girl's place was soaked again, and I was shivering with cold and a confusing mix of fear and excitement. I regretted what I'd done yet I couldn't wait to see how much money was in that shoebox.

I shut off the engine and sat there on my bike for thirty seconds or so trying to get my thoughts together. That's when the door into the kitchen opened and Cindy looked out.

"Thank God," she said. "I called you twice wondering what had happened to you."

"Rain happened," I said. "Lots of it."

"So I see. You want me to get you a towel and some dry clothes?"

"A towel and my robe, I think. Do I have time for a hot bath?"

"I'll get it started," she said. "I'll feed the girls while you're soaking."

"Thanks, baby."

"I kept praying you hadn't wrecked somewhere."

"Must have worked," I told her. She gave me that smile then that always made me feel better than any *I love you* could. It was 30 percent mouth and 70 percent eyes, and what that smile said was *I need you so so much, Russell. I need you more than I need myself.*

I tried to give her the same kind of smile back and said, "Hit the garage door button, will you, baby?"

The door grumbled and clanked down to the concrete, and only then did I start to get some breath back. How could anybody know it was me? I kept asking myself. The girl didn't know me and I didn't know her. The dog didn't know me. The only question was, had somebody come along while I was in the house who recognized my bike? I figured that was the only thing I had to worry about. That and what was going to happen to my soul. I prayed that Gee might be able to pull some strings from her end.

I finally managed to haul myself off the bike and peel off my top shirt. It was a short-sleeve chambray and felt like it weighed five pounds. The T-shirt underneath was plastered to my skin, and every time my icy fingers touched some other part of me I winced. Cindy came out then with a beach towel and the gray fleece robe the girls gave me the previous Christmas. She set those things on my workbench and grabbed the back of the T-shirt and dragged it up over my head and then wrapped the beach towel around my shoulders. "Go sit on the step and I'll take your boots off," she said.

"Sweetie, I'll do it. You don't need to be out here."

"You're practically blue," she said.

"Who knew rain in August could feel so cold?"

"It's the wind chill," she said. "Where's your raincoat? Didn't you even put it on?"

"Stupid, I know. I started out under a patch of blue sky."

"Did you think it was going to follow you the whole way home?"

I grabbed her in both arms then and pulled her close, held her to me tighter than I had in a long time. When I finally kissed the top of her head and let her go she looked up at me and said, "You almost wrecked, didn't you?"

"Why do you say that?"

"Because you're still shook up about it."

She turned to the bike then and went over to it and started studying it up close.

I said, "What are you looking for?"

"It doesn't look like you laid it down."

"I fishtailed once is all. Some idiot in a big black Land Cruiser pulled right out in front of me."

"You let him have it?" she asked.

"I was too busy trying to stay upright. By the time I got steadied, he was nothing but a couple of taillights."

She came away from the bike then, back to me, which made me feel a little easier. "Aw babe," she said, and laid a pair of warm hands on my waist. "I'm sorry you had such a nasty ride home. How was the rest of the day?"

"Good," I told her. "No problems."

She wanted to help me get the rest of my clothes off but I finally convinced her to go back in the house and let me do it. Then I sat there on the top of the three concrete steps that go up from the garage floor to the door into the kitchen, and with fingers that were still stiff and stinging I unlaced my boots and wiggled them off. My feet were the only part of me still dry.

Ever since I came home from the service I've been wearing my tan desert boots whenever I rode the bike. I told myself it was because they were a lot more comfortable than the heavier and stiffer discount-store bike boots I had, and that was true, but I think another reason they feel so right on my feet is because they keep me attached to that other time. I hated nearly every minute of my time in the Army, yet I'm grateful for it too. You can't endure as much discomfort and downright pain as a soldier does, and you sure as hell can't witness as much violence and stupidity and cruelty as we did, without it leaving its mark on you. Wearing my boots while doing one of the things I love best is my way of saying thanks to the Army, I guess. No, not to the Army really, but more to the things I experienced in the Army. I came across so many people a lot worse off than me. A world of suffering, but goodness too. A way of life I'd never imagined existed when I was growing up in Pops and Gee's house.

And that day as I took my boots off in the garage, as I held onto my dry socks with both hands and looked over at my bike dripping onto the concrete floor, it was like a switch clicked in my brain and I was looking at the cement porch of that house we searched in Iraq—the one with the boy chained up outside, same as that pit bull at the house I'd just left. He was maybe twelve, thirteen years old. Man, we talked about that boy for days afterward, always questioning ourselves. Down's Syndrome, you said. I can see him as plain as day right now, that goofy, crooked grin when he saw us coming into the yard, like we were the most exciting thing he'd ever seen. That rusty chain, maybe fifteen feet long, fastened around his ankle on one end, around a porch column at the other end. The way the chain had worn away the bottom of the column till it was nothing but a thin spindle, and us wondering how long it would take before it wore through completely, either through the column or through the poor kid's leg.

I can still see that little bed the boy had up against the porch, made from a couple of dirty blankets. And those dark eyes of his watching us coming and going—eyes full of expectation, I think.

And then we finished the search and walked away and left him there. And couldn't stop talking about him. Should we have taken him to that dilapidated hospital down the road, where he probably would have been locked in a room and forgotten about? At least he was being fed where he was. I wonder if he's still there. I wonder if the column finally wore through, and he did what? Just walked away with that chain dragging behind him?

Christ, life is hard. I wish we had set that kid free. I wish it so bad, like it could've been the best thing I did over there. But I didn't. None of us did.

And I sat there on my garage step, Spence, remembering that kid chained up like a dog, remembering that I was now no better than a common thief, and I sobbed like a baby.

The only thing that got me to stop finally was knowing Cindy or one of the girls could open the door any minute, and if they saw me sitting there crying they never would have understood why. And how could they, really? How could they know that in all my time growing up without a father and with a mother slowly dying, and in all my time in the military swallowing sand and bullshit, and in all my time in college feeling out of place and destined to fail, I had never once realized the way I did in that garage how beautiful and fucking ugly the world outside can be.

*

Anytime Cindy lays her hand between my legs while we're watching TV in bed, I know what it means. It doesn't happen very often, what with us cleaning up after dinner, then getting the girls their baths and playing with or reading to them until they fall asleep. By then we're both exhausted and know we have to get up and start again at sunrise or earlier, so the sexual part of our life usually only happens on weekends, and especially when we get the girl down the street to take our girls to a movie or the skating rink or something. In which case, I'm usually looking at Cindy a certain way long before she has to lay a finger on me.

But that night after the naked girl we were both sitting up in bed with the little TV on, and underneath the sheet she slid her hand over and laid it on my thigh. I knew if I sat there and did nothing, after a few minutes or so she'd move her pinkie finger a little, enough to touch me where it counts. In most cases, though, about thirty seconds of her hand touching my skin is enough for me, and before you know it she can tell how interested I am. And I'm always interested.

This night, though, she didn't get any reaction whatsoever when she first touched me. My head was pounding with too many thoughts, all of them bouncing around inside my skull like billiard balls. *Why* did I take that money? And what was I going to do with it now? I couldn't hide it from Cindy forever. And what if somebody at the bank said something to her about the plant closing?

Silence is the same as a lie, Gee used to say when she was trying to get me to confess to some little thing. Like who ate the candy bar supposed to be in Pops' lunch. Who left the cap off the milk bottle. Stuff that in the end was pretty easy to confess to.

But there wasn't going to be anything easy about these new confessions. I should have come out with it all right then and there. I just wasn't thinking straight. She had a hand on my thigh and I knew what she was leading up to, and I also knew I couldn't sit there and wait until she made the next move either, because she's the kind that always takes even the smallest rejection personally. I have to be very careful when it comes to that. I mean, even something like, "Honey, I'm too busy right now to listen to what your customer did today" will bring tears to her eyes. So I had to find some way of tiptoeing around letting her know I was in no mood for making love.

"We have any flu medicine in the house?" I asked.

"Aren't you feeling good, babe?"

"I've had the chills ever since I got home. And my body feels like somebody's been punching on me all day."

"There's Children's Flu and Cold," she said.

"Will that work on me?"

"I don't see why not. Maybe double up the dosage. You want me to get it for you?"

"Stay in bed, I'll get it."

I went into the bathroom and made a little noise and then I went back into the bedroom making a face and smacking my lips. She said, "What did you do, drink out of the bottle?"

"Out of the cap," I said.

"Which is now on top of the bottle."

"We've all got the same germs, baby."

"Except for the new ones you put in the medicine."

"Isn't that medicine supposed to kill those germs?"

She looked at me and shook her head but she couldn't hide the little smile.

I told her, "I'm going to make a cup of tea, see if that will warm me up while the medicine goes to work. You want one?"

She shook her head no and said, "Get something to wrap up in."

"I'll get my coat out of the closet. Is it only me, or are you cold too?"

"I'm fine. The air conditioner is set at seventy."

"It's only me then."

"Get the thermometer and I'll take your temperature."

"Watch your show. I'll be okay."

That money in my saddlebag was all I was able to think about. One minute it seemed like a birthday present waiting to be unwrapped, and the next minute like a ticking time bomb. I kept asking myself, what kind of a person are you to have done such a thing? I'd think, that girl probably can't even remember what you look like. Then I'd hear the house creak and I'd go stiff and sit there waiting for the door to be kicked in.

Plus I kept wondering about whose money it was I'd taken. I knew that girl wasn't in charge of the place. She was there to keep watch over things, her and the dog. And I guess maybe she kept watch a little too closely, so close that some of the stuff she was watching got inside her.

I'd never thought of myself as a thief before. Sure, every now and then when I was a teenager I'd sneak a couple dollars out of Pops' change jar, but I was relatively sure he knew I was doing it. He even said to me from time to time, "If you're short on jingle, go grab yourself some out of my jar." Taking ten dollars one time was probably the worst I'd ever done.

But I'd taken a lot more than that this time. And without anybody giving me permission to do so. I didn't like what that said about me. But what I didn't like even more was not being able to take care of my family.

Gee used to say that everything happens for a reason. In her mind, it was God's reason, of course, and that didn't always mean we were going to like it. Sometimes He put temptation in our path to see how we would handle it. In which case I'd failed an important test.

On the other hand, God's always been a contradiction to me. I'd say to Gee, "Doesn't God know all there is to know?"

"Of course He does. He knows every hair on your head."

"Then why doesn't He know when somebody is going to give in to a temptation? Why doesn't He stop it before it happens?"

That was the one thing she never could abide from me, questioning God's almighty wisdom. And it was the one thing I never could keep myself from doing.

Anyway, I sat in front of the TV that night, sweating in the lightest jacket I could find in the closet, until I was reasonably certain Cindy wasn't going to come downstairs to ask how I was doing. Then I shed the jacket and tried to fall asleep on the couch. But then I started thinking about that naked girl, and damn if I didn't get hard thinking about how she looked all muddy and wet in her yard.

I was so horny all of a sudden I almost got up and went back to Cindy. But then I thought what an asshole I'd be, using my wife like that. So instead I went to the little side room that was supposed to be a dining room but where the computer is set up and where most of the girls' toys always end up on the floor.

I had a good idea about what I'd seen at the house that afternoon but I wanted to be even more certain. I mean the black poster paper over all the windows, the cat piss stink of the place, the buckets full of rags in the tub. I'd never been in a meth house but I'd seen enough TV shows to have a pretty good idea. So in the Internet search box I typed *What does a meth lab look like?* Sixty seconds later I was as certain as I needed to be.

At first I felt a surge of satisfaction, as if I'd proven something important to myself. I guess you could say I was looking for a kind of justification, as if stealing from dopers is different than stealing from your neighbor the schoolteacher or the guy across town who sells antiques. For the life of me I couldn't even make up my mind about what Gee would say in a situation like this. Would she say, *Sin is sin, baby boy, no matter who you do it to or with*? Or maybe, *If you can turn evil to good, that's when you know you're doing God's will.* Or would she say, *It's what's in your heart that matters. God only cares about what's in your heart?*

If I ever had such a thing as a moral compass in my life, it had been Gee. Still is, I guess, considering how much time I spent sitting there trying to figure out what she might say to me about this.

After a while, though, it was sort of like you stepped into my head, Spence, and very politely pushed Gee aside. *Soldiers*, I could hear you saying. That was always the way you'd get things started when you had a little speech to make. And I liked hearing that word, no denial here. When you grow up not only an only child but half an orphan, and somebody you admire throws his arms around you in brotherhood, it's a powerful feeling. That word always warmed me up in an instant and made me want to do whatever you were about to suggest.

Soldiers, I could hear you saying, *'tis done what 'tis done. You can't wish it away, you can't undo it, you can't paint it over or pretend it isn't there. It's the elephant in the room—you understand what I'm saying? For the time being it might be a sleeping elephant, but elephants don't sleep forever. It's going to wake up someday and see you trying to tiptoe around it, and it's going to be pissed. It's going to reach out with its trunk and haul you in and rape the living shit out of you. And the only thing for you to do, assuming the thought of being raped by an elephant does not appeal to you, is to get busy while it's still sleeping and figure out how to get it out of your house without waking it up. Are you gonna bail and move out, let the elephant have your house? Are you gonna cut out a big circle in your floor, then hire a crane to pick up your house and move it? What's your best option here? That's what you have to figure out and figure out quick. You don't sleep, you don't eat, you don't even visit the fucking latrine until you have a plan of action. And then you execute. Maybe it's only an 80 percent solution, but a well-executed 80 percent solution is better than a 100 percent solution that comes too late. So you pull on your pants, you lace up your boots, you get the job fucking done. Period.*

The last time I looked at the blue numbers on the cable box that night, they said 4:17. Two and a half hours later I woke up to Cindy's hand on my forehead. When I looked up at her she said, "You don't seem to have a temperature anymore. You feeling okay?"

"Better," I said, and sat up. "Yeah, I'm good now."

"I'll call Jake if you want me to."

"I'm good," I said. "You mind if I take the truck today?"

*

That day, the day after the incident with the girl, Jake seemed to be avoiding me most of the day, which was fine with me, seeing as how it was all I could do to keep from falling into a piece of equipment, not only from lack of sleep but because my mind was working elsewhere. And I found every excuse I could to stay out of the office. We couldn't even look each other in the eye. He was ashamed of having made the best decision he could, and I was ashamed for making the worst.

My most immediate problem was what to do with the money. For the time being it was locked in the toolbox in the bed of my truck, but I wasn't comfortable keeping it there. What if Cindy or I had an accident and the truck had to be towed? What if the truck got stolen?

I mean, maybe those dopers had so much money that they never even counted it. Maybe they never pulled back that shower curtain except to dump more bundles of cash into a box. Yeah, and maybe the earth really is flat and we don't know it yet.

I was betting those dopers knew to a dollar how much they had. I mean why else does a person go into that line of work except for the money? They probably even knew to a dollar how much was missing, which was more than I could say for myself. I hadn't even been able to bring myself to count it yet.

Anyway, by midafternoon I'd run through every possible scenario I could come up with. The way I figured, I had two things to accomplish. One was to get that money where it wasn't going to be found until I could decide what to do with it. The other was to distract the dopers, maybe for a good long time, from launching an investigation into the whereabouts of their money.

The reason I'd told Cindy I needed the truck that day was so I could go check on Pops after work. And she said, "You'll see him Sunday. Can't it wait till then?" Which caused me to have to make up another lie. I told her I'd had a bad dream about him and I couldn't get it out of my head. So she made plans during the day for another teller who lived not far from us to give her a ride home in the evening. Meantime she called the daycare and let them know I'd be a half hour or so late picking up the girls.

So after work I went to the dollar store in town, then straight to the Brookside seniors' home. Pops was in the dining room when I got there, halfway through his meatloaf. I sneaked up behind him and slipped the bag of chocolate-covered peanuts onto the table while he was talking to the old guy sitting beside him. Pops didn't notice the peanuts till he went for another forkful of meatloaf. He looked at the bag for a few seconds, then he laid down his fork. "Screw this mystery meat," he said. "I been blessed with some manna from Heaven."

I never could surprise Pops, no matter how many times I tried. So I gave his shoulder a squeeze, then slid around to an empty chair. He never even looked at me till he had the bag open and a pile of chocolate-covered peanuts dumped out onto a saucer. Then he popped a piece of candy in his mouth and looked up at me and grinned. "Christmas came early this year," he said.

I said, "You think maybe you should finish your dinner first, Pops?"

"I think maybe you should finish it," he said. "Then you'll see why I don't plan to."

The two other guys at his table both laughed, and neither one of them said no thanks when Pops passed the bag around. He asked about Cindy and the girls and how everything was going, and I asked the same, and then he smiled at me and waited.

So I said, "Would you mind if I stored the bike out in your unit this winter?"

"Why would I mind?" he said. "You get another car already?"

"Thinking about it," I said. "I got caught in that cloudburst yesterday. Nearly laid the bike down. It got me thinking that maybe it's time I stopped riding it so much."

"Long past time, if you ask me." By then he was already fumbling with the key chain on his belt loop. It still had eight or nine keys attached to it. It took him a while to get the right chain off the metal loop and hand it to me.

"You're going to have to move some things around in there," he said.

"That's what I want to do tomorrow. I'm not quite ready to put the bike away yet."

"I'd let you have the Lumina, but Art got us hooked up with a couple of nurse's aides for tomorrow night. We're taking them to the drive-in."

I looked across the table at Art. He has the baggiest old hound-dog eyes I've ever seen on a man. He shook his head no.

Pops said, "They claim the smell of Bengay turns them on. I plan to find out if that's true or not."

I said, "You better hope Gee isn't watching."

"I already took care of that," he said. "I lined the Lumina's ceiling with tinfoil."

Everybody else laughed a long time at that one, and I smiled too, but my stomach felt like I'd swallowed a brick. Since waking up I'd already lied to two of the four people I loved most in the world.

I stayed with Pops a few minutes longer, but made my goodbyes as soon as I could. When I stood up, he crimped shut the top of his candy bag and handed it to me. "Stick these in my fridge on your way out. I don't like the way Art and T.A. are eyeballing them."

The dining room is at the rear of the building, so I had to walk past a dozen or so rooms to get to the front door again. All of the rooms are alike, maybe 15 × 12, a bed, a couple of chairs, a dresser and TV and a bathroom. For obvious reasons, the residents aren't allowed to cook in their rooms, but lots of them, like Pops, keep a little refrigerator filled with whatever they like.

It was only after I put the candy away and noticed the telephone on top of Pops' fridge that I thought of what to do next. I wasn't going to use Pops' phone, that was too dangerous, but there are lots of other phones in the building too, one in nearly every room, in fact. And as far as I could tell, every resident in that wing, plus all the attendants, were in the dining room.

I picked the library because it's down a side hallway away from the front desk. The front desk was empty at the moment but there was no telling how long that would last. Plus the public restrooms are across from the library, so if anybody looked up from the front desk to see me approaching, she'd probably think I'd been in the men's room.

I was in and out of the library in less than two minutes. Dialed 911, told the operator there was a meth lab out on Route 218 about six miles north of town, little white cottage on the east side of the road, pit bull chained to a tree in the front yard. I didn't even give her a chance to ask my name or anything else.

Then I was back behind the wheel and driving. I thought about stopping long enough to throw up, but then I swallowed it down. I still had things to do.

First place I stopped was the little hardware store down from the Dollar General, where I made myself a copy of the key to Pops' storage unit. Then I drove out of town to the storage place. I got the big LED flashlight from my toolbox, plus a utility knife, a roll of duct tape, and the shoebox full of cash. Then I unlocked the unit, went inside and pulled down the door.

By this time I knew where I should put the money. Even if Pops came into the unit for some reason, and I had the feeling that maybe sometimes he did, probably to sit by himself awhile and be with those old things and all the memories in them. I mean I had no proof he ever did that, but I saw Pops and me as alike in many ways, and I knew if I was him, on his own now for the first time in fifty-some years, living surrounded by sickness and idleness and slow-moving people on the fast track to death, I would need a place like this to get away to every now and then, a place where it's easier to remember what you used to have. Hell, I'd probably move my bed and mini fridge in. In a way it would be a lot like dying the way those old pharaohs did, surrounded by all the things you would drag up into Heaven with you.

But the one thing in here I figured he would leave alone was his MISCELLANEOUS box. You don't use half a roll of duct tape sealing up a box if you plan to open it frequently.

But first I counted the money. All this time I'd been trying to keep numbers out of my head, but of course I'd been a miserable failure at it. And for some reason, fifty thousand was the number that kept flashing like a neon sign in my brain. Then I'd think, naw, maybe ten, fifteen at the most, but that neon sign had its own power source and the light had been impossible to extinguish.

The cash was in bundles held together by rubber bands. The bundles were of various thicknesses, depending on the mix of denominations. Tens were rare, but twenties weren't. There was no shortage of fifties or hundreds either. I only had to count through four bundles to realize that every bundle held five thousand dollars. And there were three layers of bundles in the shoebox. With four bundles in each layer. Plus six more bundles stuffed around the edges to make the layers snug.

I am well aware that for lots of people in this world, ninety thousand dollars is no big deal. Some people make more than that in a year. Some actors and athletes make that much for an hour or two of work. But I'm not one of those people.

For me, ninety thousand dollars represents two years of dust-sucking work. Three years if you factor in the taxes.

It took a while for the dizziness to pass. I had meant to get all this done quickly, cause I still had the girls to pick up. But for several minutes at least, I couldn't move except to shiver and rock back and forth with my hands squeezing my knees.

*

No matter how well a person plans, there's always something you don't plan for. I'm talking now about my plan for hiding the cash I'd stolen in Pops' MISCELLANEOUS box. It had never occurred to me there wouldn't be enough room in the box for all that money. I sliced through the sealing tape, one neat cut at each end and another down the middle seam on top, and there was all this stuff I'd never expected.

Some of it looked like junk to me at first, though I'm sure Pops thought there was some value to it, or else he wouldn't have packed it away for me. Two old Kodak cameras that must've been from the thirties or forties. Three tiny glass deer, a buck and a doe and a fawn all glued to the same glass base, which I had given Mom on her last Mother's Day. Pops had given me the five dollars to buy it when we were at Woolworth's one time, but I'd insisted on holding it in my hands on the ride home, and the thing was so delicate I accidentally broke the buck right off the stand. I could barely breathe I was crying so hard, but Pops glued it back in place when we got home, and as far as I know, Mom never once suspected it had ever been broken.

Then there was a pair of bronzed baby shoes, which I assumed had once been worn by my mother, or maybe by me. Then the heavy-handled knife with a thick ten-inch blade I found in Pops' closet when I was fourteen, and carried around with me for a week, shoved down into my waistband, until a teacher caught me showing it to a girl and called Pops about it.

Standing on its side in a corner of the cardboard box was Pops' black fireproof box with the key in the lock, and inside was his will and gold watch, his discharge papers and Purple Cross, three silver dollars and a wallet holding four silver certificates, three two-dollar bills, and six bills all marked with the words Ngan-Hang Quoc-Gia Viet-Nam. The twenties had a picture of a big, impressive building on them, and the 500s had a tiger, and the 1000s had skinny little men riding elephants. I thought it was sort of funny in a touching kind of way to find that Vietnamese money, because when I came home from the desert I handed Pops a little wad of the old, worthless dinar with Saddam's picture on it, and I told him what he'd always told me when he handed me a dollar when I was little, "Don't spend it all in one place."

There was also his change jar, a half-gallon Mason jar, and it was filled to the lid with coins of every denomination. The box holding his Harrington & Richardson .22 revolver in his USMC holster was propped up on its side against the jar. Pops taught me to shoot with that gun. We practiced on bottles and cans and rats at the dump until he was convinced I knew how to handle a gun properly. After each trip to the dump he'd watch while I cleaned out the barrel, then the revolver would go back into the holster and under his pillow. Sometimes when he wasn't around I'd sit on his bed and just hold it. It felt so heavy and solid and, I don't know, reassuring in my hands. Like I was holding his hand, in a way, which we stopped doing when I hit thirteen or so.

In that same box was his favorite Craftsman wrench set, six heavy wrenches, still gleaming and without a scratch. A small, heavy purse of Gee's I used to play with all the time, because I liked the feel of it so much. It was made out of tiny metal overlapping plates that shimmered like fish scales. Gee said it had belonged to her own mother, and came from the Roaring Twenties.

Three framed 5 × 7s, one of Pops, one of Gee, and one of my mother, each of them holding me as a baby, all taken on the same day, I guess, seeing as how I was wrapped up in the same blue blanket and had the same goofy smile on my face each time.

Another 5 × 7 that, even as a kid, used to break my heart when I looked at it, and it was impossible not to look at it every day, seeing as how it always sat on top of the television set. It was a picture of Gee when she was only nineteen years old, and on her lap was a chubby little baby boy who looked a lot like a cherub out of a religious painting. This was a photo Gee had taken while Pops was in Asia. It would have been the first look he had of his son. And not long after that it became the only look he'd ever have of him, because the little boy, David Jr., died of pneumonia a few months after the photo was taken.

Back before Mom had me, she asked a friend of hers to use an old photo of Pops in his dress blues, and somehow combine it with the photo of Gee and little Davy. I don't know if there was such a thing as Photoshop back then or not, but I do know that Gee cherished that photo of the three of them, even though if you got close up the photo of Pops looked like a kind of cutout superimposed behind Gee's right shoulder. Still, when Pops and Gee took Mom and me in, it was almost like we were a family of five instead of four. Hardly a night passed that Mom didn't say "Goodnight, Davy," on her way up the stairs. Later, when she wasn't able to climb the stairs anymore and slept on a roll-up bed in the dining room, I'd sometimes hear her talking in the middle of the night, and the only thing that kept me from being scared was telling myself she was talking to her brother, Davy.

And there was other stuff in that box too, every piece wrapped in its own sheet of Bubble Wrap, all those worthless, priceless pieces of the past the four of us had shared. I was weak and shaky and teary-eyed from looking at them, even the ones I didn't remember ever seeing before, and at the same time I felt all dirty and despicable because of those bundles of cash at my feet.

Then my phone beeped in my pocket and nearly shocked me out of my skin. It was a text from the daycare center, reminding me that they closed at six and would I be coming soon? I texted back *B there in 10.* Then I repacked the box and covered the cut tape with strips of fresh duct tape, one strip over each cut because I knew I would be back to look inside that box again.

Then it was a matter of finding somewhere else to put the money. I started looking at the furniture pushed up against the wall. The secretary and dresser had lots of empty drawers, but how bright would it be to dump the money in there?

I finally settled on the rolltop desk, especially after I found a key in the little drawer underneath the rolltop part. The key was for locking the rolltop down, which was exactly what I did after I'd stuffed each of the six pigeonholes with bundles of cash, then stacked the rest of the bundles in front of the pigeonholes. Afterward I pocketed the key to guarantee that if maybe Pops ever got the idea of locking something of his own in there, he wouldn't be able to get the top up.

Before leaving I checked and double-checked and triple-checked everything I'd touched, and felt for that key in my pocket at least a half-dozen times, making sure it hadn't evaporated, I guess. Then I locked up the unit, shook the padlock as hard as I could to make sure it was secure, and climbed back into the truck with nothing in my hands but a smashed-down shoebox.

I backtracked a couple of miles, using those few minutes to calm myself down as much as I could before I picked up the girls. I pulled over a block from the daycare to stuff the shoebox into a trash can, then drove forward and parked again and apologized to Anita, a college girl who had stayed late and was keeping the girls entertained with a game of Chutes and Ladders.

I was still out of breath and nauseated when I pulled into the garage at home and unbuckled Emma from her car seat. Then Dani climbed out and sniffed the air and squealed, "I smell pasgetti!," and I couldn't keep it down any longer. I hustled outside around the corner of the garage and hoped the neighbors weren't watching while I puked into the grass.

*

Sunday mornings I usually stay in bed with Cindy, snuggling and talking about whatever, until we hear the girls making noise. But that next Sunday wasn't typical, and I was awake before dawn, even though I'd spent most of the night jerking awake at the slightest sound, some of them probably not even real. I slipped out of bed and dressed and put on a pot of coffee, and while the coffee was dripping into the pot I walked out our street to the intersection, where there's one of those glass boxes with newspapers in it.

I bought a copy and checked out the entire front page before I got back home. Nothing. Then I laid it out on the counter and drank my coffee and went through the paper from front to back. By the time I got to the last page, the coffee tasted sour going down and even worse in my stomach.

Around here, it's big news if the police shut down a meth lab. The whole county is basically a bunch of small towns and villages, a lot of two- or three-man police forces whose biggest excitement is breaking up a bar fight or a domestic disturbance. Early last spring a van

49

with fourteen illegals in it was stopped along the interstate that runs through the northern part of the county, and before long that part of the highway looked like a state trooper convention. I swear that if it had happened at night instead of in the afternoon, the glow from all those flashing red and blue lights would have painted the sky like the aurora borealis. It was all anybody could talk about for at least a week.

So when the Sunday paper had not a word in it about a meth lab being raided out along Route 218, I knew that despite the call I made from the nursing home, no raid had taken place, or one had but nobody was arrested. And every implication of that was sickening. I knew I had to do something, but what?

That morning dragged on forever, though even now I can't remember any of it, except that it seemed an eternity before the girls finished lunch and I came up with a plan. I said, "How about after your mom and me clean up the dishes, we go get G-paw and take him out for an ice cream?" Of course, that suggestion had the effect I knew it would, at least from the girls.

Cindy said, "I thought you said you were going to mow the yard today. And then you'd bring him over for a barbecue tonight. Remember?"

She could tell by the look on my face that I had no idea what she was talking about.

"I mentioned it Friday when you wanted the truck for the day," she said. "Don't you remember? It was your idea last Monday, Tuesday night. You said if the weather was good on Sunday, today, which it is, you wanted to mow the yard and then bring Pops over to spend the day with us. That's why there's a rack of ribs and four chicken breasts thawing out in the refrigerator right now."

The girls started chanting, "Ice cream! Ice cream!" And I told them, "Hush now, I can't think."

Cindy said, "We can do it some other time if you want, it's up to you. But remember that Dani starts first grade the day after Labor Day, and I haven't had a chance to get her any school supplies yet, and both girls need a couple of outfits and new shoes. I was planning on going to the outlets next weekend to do all that. Which means putting off a barbecue until, what—the second weekend in September?"

I sat there blinking, feeling stupid, unable to put a single clear thought together.

"Ice cream," Dani said in a loud whisper.

So Emma, of course, had to scream it at the top of her lungs. "Ice creeeeem!"

And at the sound of that shriek I jerked. I practically jumped out of my chair.

Cindy studied me for a few seconds. "You all right?" she asked. "Are you still not feeling well?"

I took a couple of breaths, then I gave them all what even I knew was a phony smile. "Let's do this, okay, guys? I'll get started on the yard while you two help your mom out in here. I want your rooms cleaned too before Pops gets here. And if you do everything Mom asks you to, when I go pick up Pops I'll bring home some of that cookie dough ice cream you like."

"Yeah!" Dani said, and Emma grinned and bounced up and down in her booster seat.

I asked Cindy, "Is that okay?"

"Sounds like a plan. You mind getting the ice cream at the Giant Eagle down the road from Pops? They have those sweet Hawaiian rolls he likes."

"Sure. Make me a list."

"The girls and I will make potato salad. Can you buy another side, something without mayonnaise in it?"

I pushed myself away from the table, put my hands on the edge of the table and stood up. "Put it on the list so I don't forget."

She followed me out into the pantry and stopped me before I went out the back door. "Hey," she said, just loud enough for her and me.

I turned.

"Are you all right?"

I smiled again. "Don't I look all right?"

"No, you don't. You look like you need to go back to bed."

"My stomach's a little queasy, that's all."

"Why don't you forget about the yard for today?"

"Well if you have a magic wand you can wave over it, you be my guest."

I knew the moment I said it, it was not a good thing to say. We don't talk that way to each other. I think we both try to be as gentle with each other and the girls as we can. Cindy has a special aversion to sarcasm, which, as she has told me many times, especially after one of her mother's visits, she considers "the lowest form of humor."

And now I couldn't bear that look in her eyes. I stepped back and put my arms around her and pulled her up against me. "I'm sorry, baby. I just . . ."

She rubbed her hand around in a circle between my shoulder blades. "Not enough sleep and an upset stomach, I know. Let's forget about a barbecue today."

"I'll be fine," I told her. "I really do want Pops to get a little sunshine before it's gone for the year."

"You're going to end up making yourself even sicker."

"I'm a big boy," I told her, and I kissed the side of her head.

"A big stubborn baby," she said, but she gave me another squeeze before she let go and turned back to the kitchen.

The yard that day seemed twice as big as usual. I kept wanting to turn the lawn tractor out onto the sidewalk, and keep on going until there was nowhere left to go.

While I was mowing and dreaming of driving straight into the ocean, Cindy called Pops to remind him about the barbecue and ask what time he wanted to come over. And Pops, being Pops, said something like, "Let me have my secretary check the schedule. I know I have a board meeting at eleven, I address Congress at twelve, and from one to two I'm supposed to go skinny-dipping with Lucy Liu. But I can put those off until tomorrow, especially for some of Russell's burned spareribs."

Cindy thought Pops was hilarious. He never made fun of other people, only himself. And sometimes politicians and actors and million-aire athletes. But the real people, as he called the rest of us, he left alone.

Anyway, they decided on 3:00 p.m., and Cindy talked him out of driving over himself, said it would be a waste of gas since I had to go right past his place anyway to pick up a few things from the store. "And of course," Cindy told me, "he argued that it would be a waste of even more gas for you to drive the whole way over there when he could go to the store himself."

I hadn't noticed any major problems with his driving skills up till then except for the slowness and a tendency to drift to the right, which he blamed on the Lumina being out of alignment, but Cindy has always been very protective of him and seems to worry about him even more than I do. And the thing about Pops is, if a man asks him to do some-thing, Pops will argue until kingdom come, but if a woman asks, he's eventually going to end up doing whatever she wants.

So after I showered and made a quick stop at Giant Eagle, I went to pick him up—and there he was waiting on the bench out front of Brookside, exactly like I knew he would be. He climbed in and buckled up, and I said, "Lucy Liu, Pops?"

"Don't pretend you don't think she's a beautiful woman."

"I never said that."

"Name a woman more beautiful than her."

"I don't know. Maybe, uh . . ."

"Don't even try, son. It's an exercise in futility."

Being around Pops always made me feel better. All day long my head had felt like it was being squeezed in a vise, while at the same time it was swelling from the inside out. But now, for the first time in forty-eight hours, the pressure let up a little bit.

There was something about Pops' attitude, I guess, even when he wasn't saying anything. I mean there he was almost eighty years old, and still wearing the sleeves of his T-shirt rolled up so as to show off his biceps. Within an hour he'd be doing one-handed push-ups in the yard with one of the girls riding on his back. I used to marvel at the way he'd make a speed bag sing. He was the toughest old bird I knew, and yet the softest when it came down to his family. I guess it's fair to say he was everything I wanted to be, but now believed I never could. Even if I gave the money back, I would always be a thief. I would be like the glass deer I broke and then glued back into place. Maybe nobody else ever noticed the damage, but I always knew it was there. And I was always worried that sooner or later somebody else would see it too.

On the way out of town I played with the idea of telling him everything. But then he said, "You get that furniture moved around out in the unit?"

I nodded, because I couldn't bear to lie to him out loud. "There's your key in the console," I told him. "Thanks a lot."

"Is there enough room for your bike?"

"Plenty," I said.

"Things must be going pretty good at the plant if you're thinking about getting a car."

"Real well," I told him. Then, "Hey, by the way, do me a favor and don't mention anything about a new car to Cindy. I was going to surprise her with the idea, but in fact I'm having second thoughts about putting the bike away so early. I can't let one little skid spook me into not riding. Not with at least two more months of good riding left."

"It's not the skid that's important, though. It's those babies of yours."

"I know, Pops. I know."

I could feel him looking at me a couple of times, but he didn't say anything more.

Then I saw the Get-Go up ahead, and that's when I decided I couldn't wait until later to satisfy my curiosity. I had planned to run past the naked girl's house after I took Pops home that night, but it would be dark by then and besides I would probably be half-crazy with nervousness wondering if the place had gotten busted or not.

So I flipped my turn signal on and said, "You mind if we take the scenic route home?"

"As long as you can keep it to a minimum," he said. "Too much scenery might throw me into a seizure of some kind."

Not only was there no police tape around the little house, but the windows weren't blacked out now, and the pit bull was chained up closer to the house and sleeping in the shade by the front steps. It didn't make any sense to me.

Pops said, "What are you slowing down for? You're driving like me now."

"This is where I almost lost it on the bike. Car pulled out in front of me."

"Out of that driveway?"

"That's the one. You have any idea who lives in that place?"

"Somebody who needs a couple of driving lessons, is all I know. What kind of car was it?"

"To be honest with you, Pops, I don't even remember. I hit the brakes and started fishtailing. By the time I got the bike straightened out, the car was long gone."

"Well," he said, looking out at the trees now, "let's hope this little excursion past the scene of the crime has exorcised your demons."

We were still a couple of miles from home when I said to him, "Hey, you know what I all of sudden remembered when I was out in your unit yesterday? Those times you took me shooting in the dump."

Pops smiled and looked out the window. "That old dump's long gone now. Some fella put a motel or something up along the edge of that ravine."

"Bed and breakfast," I told him. "Built to look like a little English castle. You can't even tell it's all modular construction. Went up in four days."

"Probably took longer than that to clean out the dump."

"Probably did." I let a few seconds pass. "Hey, whatever happened to that gun we used? That old revolver."

He looked at me and grinned.

"What?" I said.

"It's in the MISCELLANEOUS box. It's yours now."

"No kidding?" I said. "Does it still work?"

"Why wouldn't it?"

"Didn't you tell me once that Gee bought it for you way back when? It must be an antique by now."

"I'm an antique and I still work," he said. "I drive a little slower is all."

"Yeah but you still get to go skinny-dipping with Lucy Liu."

"Every night," he said. "I pop in that *Charlie's Angels* DVD, turn out the lights, and then Lucy and me head off to the swimming hole."

I put on the turn signal and turned down the cul-de-sac. "These are things I'd rather not hear about, Pops."

"Just you wait," he said.

I pulled up in front of the garage. I knew the girls would come running out any second now. "Did you even have to register your firearms back in those days?" I asked.

"Probably supposed to," he said, and then he popped open his door, because here came the girls, laughing and squealing.

*

You know how they say if you fool around with a Ouija board you open up a door that any spirit good or bad can come in? And that the ones that most want to get at you are the bad ones? I'm wondering if the same holds true for bad stuff in general. Like if I'm in a hurry to get to the bathroom some morning and I stub my toe on the dresser. An hour later I might spill coffee all over the floor, then scrape a fender pulling the truck out of the garage, then accidentally run over the garbage can because I'm so ticked off about the fender. It's like that book Dani loves so much, something about a series of unfortunate events. And let's say the first event was something a whole lot worse than stubbing a toe, something major, something like stealing a significant amount of money. Are even bigger and badder things now likely to follow in the wake of that?

By doing that one bad thing, did I maybe open up my life to a whole world of bigger and nastier trouble?

I'm going to have to answer yes to that.

*

So the weekend passed, and Monday morning I kept telling myself to say something to Cindy about the plant closing. Sooner or later she was going to hear about it at the bank. Thing is, I knew how she would react. She can go into panic mode over the tiniest thing. Why put her through that sooner than necessary? Fridays were the busiest days of the week at the bank, so maybe I could squeak by until then.

I knew I was just kidding myself, but I wanted so bad to believe it. I wanted to believe I could hide the truth from her until I found another job. I'd been spending a lot of my time at the plant searching online and then calling up potential employers and e-mailing my résumé, but I still didn't have any interviews lined up. I was seriously considering driving around to the fast food places to see if any of them was hiring.

And when I wasn't all stressed out about a job, all I could think about was stealing that money. I wanted to believe the people from that meth house were so screwed up on their own product that they might never even notice the missing box. And what if they did notice it? How was anybody going to connect me to its disappearance? The girl had been too doped up to see straight, and dogs can't talk.

Hoping for the best like that was the only way I could keep myself from going crazy.

It's funny how foolish a man can become when he gets himself stuck in an impossible situation.

So I kept my mouth shut, kissed Cindy and the girls goodbye, and headed off to work like it was just another day. At the plant, though, everybody's attitude had gone way past sour. We had four guys running equipment, and they were all at least ten years older than me, in fact two of them were closing in on sixty. But that didn't keep them from giving me an earful at some point during the day, and they all had more or less the same thing to say. We should've had more warning than this. There's no such thing as loyalty anymore. A man works his entire freaking life . . . I never thought Jake would treat us like this . . . Those damn Chinamen are taking over the world . . . When's the government going to do something about what's happening to this country?

And all I could do was to nod and say the same thing over and over again. I know. I agree. Me too. It's not right. I'm in the same boat you are.

Truth is, I wasn't in the same boat at all. As far as I could tell, I wasn't even in a boat. What I felt like was that first day of my and Cindy's honeymoon when we went to Ocean City for a long weekend. While she was laying there sunning herself, I went swimming so far out that the only way I could see our blue patch of beach towel with the tiny dot of yellow from her swimsuit was when a wave lifted me up. By the time I realized that the patch of blue was getting smaller and smaller and farther and farther to my left, and that without swimming a stroke

I was moving past that long fishing pier, I felt more used up than on the first day of basic. At first I panicked and started swimming straight toward the shore, but all that accomplished was to wear myself out even more. When I finally remembered that the only way out of a riptide is to swim to the side instead of into it, I was a good three hundred yards from Cindy and fairly certain I was never going to see her again.

Maybe a half hour later I came trudging up the beach toward where Cindy was sitting up now and staring out at the horizon. Every breath felt like broken glass going down my throat. My arms felt like they were going to drop off, and my legs felt like they were filled with cement.

I dropped down beside her and laid out on my back. She said, "There you are. You take a walk down the beach?"

"Long walk," I said.

"You weren't looking at all the pretty girls, were you?"

"Not all of them," I said.

"Well, you better not have worn yourself out," she told me. "I have plans for you when we get back to our room."

And that's exactly how I felt when I got home after work Monday night after making a stop at the storage unit, that same combination of total exhaustion and the dread of an impending duty I was in no mood to undertake. And then all that misery tripled when I went into the kitchen to see Cindy's father standing there at the kitchen sink, blowing cigarette smoke out the window screen.

"Hey there, Russell," he said, as if we'd seen each other a few days before and not years ago. He took another long drag from the cigarette, then turned on the tap and flushed the butt down the garbage disposal.

I said, "You don't put paper down a garbage disposal. It's not made for that."

He grinned and said, "You put paper down the toilet, don't you? And it all ends up in the same place."

"More important," I told him, "there's no smoking in this house."

"I blew it out the window," he said.

"There is no smoking. In this house."

"You're the king of the castle," he said. "So how's everything been going?"

Right then I knew it was a good idea I'd left Pops' revolver in the saddlebag and hadn't carried it inside with me. I turned and went into the living room in search of Cindy and the girls.

All three of them were in Cindy's and my bed. The girls were sitting up against the headboard on either side of Cindy, watching some Nickelodeon show on the little TV on the dresser. Cindy was laying on her back with her arms crossed over her chest, hands tucked into her armpits and her feet crossed at the ankle. She looked at me in a kind of a squint and her mouth never twitched out of its hard, thin line.

The girls said "Hi, Daddy," but otherwise they were doing their best to mimic their mother.

I came inside and sat on the edge beside Emma. "What's this?" I asked. "A *SpongeBob* convention?"

She said, "It's not *SpongeBob*, it's *T.U.F.F. Puppy*," and Dani said, "Grandpa's here."

"Don't call him that," Cindy told her.

I asked the girls a couple of questions about how their day was, then I suggested they go to their own bedroom and decide where they wanted to go out for dinner. "No fast food," I told them. "You two go decide. Either the buffet at KFC, or pizza and salads at Joe's."

"Pizza!" Emma said.

"Go talk it over, okay? You both have to agree. I'll come see you in a minute or two. Please close the door on your way out."

The moment the bedroom door was closed, Cindy jerked her head around to look at me and said, "I did not invite him here."

"I'd never think you did. Not unless you were standing here with a smoking gun in your hand."

"I wish I had one," she said.

All I could do was nod. Then, "What brings him here out of the blue all of a sudden?"

"Claims he came to see his grandchildren. What a bunch of bull that is."

I sat there thinking the same thing I always thought on the other occasions I had seen her father. I never understood how Cindy could be so decisive and even tough when necessary, with me and everybody else, yet so, I don't know, crumpled up and passive around her father. Early on I had asked her a couple times why she could barely speak to him without gritting her teeth, but the most she'd ever tell me was, "I hate him. I hate the sight of him. He makes me sick to my stomach."

Of course I had a fairly good idea why a girl would hate her father with that kind of intensity, but I long ago decided to respect her privacy about it. I figure if she wants to tell me anything, she'll tell me. I don't have to know every little secret to love her. And I hope she feels the same way about me.

"What do you want me to do?" I said.

And she said, "I want him out of my house."

I didn't even pause on my way through the kitchen. "Out back," I told him.

I stood up against the rail on our little patio deck, looking out into the yard. When your wife hates her father as much as Cindy did, I think it's natural for her husband to hate him too, even if he's not sure why. From what I'd heard, a lot of people seemed to like Donnie, claimed he was a friendly, decent guy. All I knew about him was that he appeared to change jobs a lot, and that he struck me as a cross between a used car salesman and a lawyer. He had the same soft way of talking and same greasy smile I'd encountered in men of those professions, though I'd dealt with a lot more used car salesmen than lawyers.

Truth is the only lawyer I knew was a guy who lived down the road from us in the first house on our street. He had a sign out in his yard that said **William Graybill, Attorney at Law**. The first time Cindy and I ever came down that street, looking for a house to buy, I had pulled the bike over right at his curb so that Cindy could look at the piece of paper in her jeans pocket that had the address on it. While we were checking the address with the house numbers, he comes walking up beside us.

"Can I help you?" he said, and not in any friendly kind of way. More like we were trespassing on his property instead of sitting on the side of a public street.

"No thanks," I told him. "We're looking for a house that's for sale."

"End of the cul-de-sac," he said. He was talking to me but smiling now at Cindy.

Then he walked up closer to her, still smiling like he was running for governor or something. "Is that a wedding ring on your hand?" he asked her. "You don't look old enough to date yet, let alone to be tied down and married."

I was about to let the guy know how sleazy he was, flirting with a man's wife right in front of him, but Cindy beat me to it. She looked him dead in the eye and gave his smile right back at him.

"Married with two children," she told him. "And couldn't be happier about it. You wouldn't believe how many slimy old creepers have been hitting on me while my husband was fighting in Iraq. Thank God that's over with. I mean I don't like that violent temper he's got, but it does come in handy sometimes, you know?"

His smile turned a little sickly then, which brought me no end of pleasure.

But that was over eight months ago, and now I'm standing on the deck, not even wanting to look her father in the face because I'm afraid I might haul off and punch him. Instead I study my grass for half a minute. Then I say, "So what are you doing here, Donnie?"

"I came to see my grandchildren. Is it okay if I smoke out here?"

"No," I told him. "And your oldest grandchild is seven years old. She's seen you twice so far."

"Okay," he says. "Truth is, I'm hoping to make things up with Janice. Figured if I could get Cindy's blessing on it, she might put a good word in for me."

"I'm fairly certain you can add 'blessing' and 'good word' to the long list of things you are never going to get from Cindy."

"I don't expect it to happen overnight," he says.

"And where did you plan to camp out while you're working on this miracle?"

"I guess I was hoping for an invitation from somebody with an extra room."

I nodded. I thought about it. And then I turned to finally look him in the eye. "How'd you get here, by the way? No vehicle, no luggage?"

"Car's a couple streets over at the convenience store."

"Well, I'll tell you what," I said. "You go get your car. Then drive on out to the interstate. Six motels within a quarter mile of each other. Lots of empty rooms out there."

*

Here's another thing I've observed. I think it's part of Murphy's Law. If it isn't, it should be. It's the fact that when you have something important to do, something like figuring out whether or not to tell your wife you're going to be unemployed soon—and whether or not to tell her about something very stupid you did—and figuring out why that meth lab out on 218 showed no sign of being raided—and figuring out what to do with all the stolen money crammed into your grandmother's antique desk—and where to hide the probably unregistered .22 revolver now in your saddlebag—and figuring out why you felt compelled to take it in the first place—all while taking your family out to dinner and pretending like nothing's wrong—then along comes something else you have to deal with first, like chasing your father-in-law away and trying to soothe your wife's mood while the kids fight over whether to get pepperoni or not on the pizza.

On second thought, Spence, forget about Murphy's Law. It should be one of the laws of physics: A body at rest tends to stay at rest until acted upon by a naked lady dancing in the rain. After that, it's going to be sandstorms and IEDs all the way to the end.

*

Any parent who is trying to be a good parent knows that, for most of every day, their own interests have to be put on hold while the kids' needs and interests are tended. Which meant that Cindy and I didn't get to talk about her father's surprise appearance until we were in bed that night. I told her how my little conversation with him had gone, and she was furious.

"No way in hell is that going to happen," she said. I'd heard her swear maybe ten times in our entire marriage. "No way in hell is he getting back with my mother."

"Do you know for sure she doesn't want to? Has she told you that?"

"It doesn't matter whether she wants to or not. I'll never let it happen."

"But if she wants to—"

"It doesn't matter what she thinks she wants, Russell! Why are you fighting me on this? You should be supporting me right now."

"Baby, I'm not fighting you. It's just that . . ."

"What? It's just that what?"

I thought of a couple questions I could ask her, but it didn't seem a good time, considering how worked up she was already. "Nothing, baby. I'm sorry. I'm behind you all the way, you know that."

"You should be," she said, and then leaned over against me, laid her head on my chest and let her hand rest on my stomach.

We stayed like that for a couple minutes, me not moving except to stroke her hair every once in a while. It had taken me a while to learn to be quiet like that with her. Back when we first got married, I thought it was my job to solve all of her problems, so anytime she would bring something up, I would add my two cents by saying, "Maybe you should do this," or "Have you thought about trying that?" Then one day she came right out and told me what she thought of my suggestions. "I don't need you to *fix* everything, Russell. Telling you what's bothering me doesn't mean I want you to *fix* it." She kept hitting the word "fix" like it was something dirty.

"Okay," I said. "Then I guess I don't know what it is you do want me to do."

"Sometimes all I want is for you to listen," she said.

So that's what I'd been trying to do unless she comes right out and asks for my opinion. It isn't easy.

After a while that night she started talking about one of the other bank tellers, a woman named Theresa whose thirty-six-year-old son still lived with her and had gotten some twenty-year-old who worked at the mall pregnant. Talking about somebody else's problems seemed to calm Cindy down.

"The thing is, the girl wants to have the baby and get married, but Theresa's son works part-time at best as a substitute teacher."

"The son doesn't want to get married?"

"He's almost forty years old and living with his mother. What do you think?"

"Sounds like maybe Theresa's going to have a couple more mouths to feed."

"Actually she's thinking very seriously about transferring her savings to a bank in Mexico or some island somewhere, then packing up and retiring. Leave her son to either grow up or else stew in his own juices, she said."

"That's how she put it—stew in his own juices? That's pretty clever."

"Umhmm," Cindy said, and moved her fingertips in a circle atop my chest.

I waited until I was sure she didn't want to say any more about it. Then I said, "By the way, I've been meaning to ask you. After I dropped Pops off yesterday, one of the other residents stopped me as I was headed for the door. He wanted my advice on what to do with all the cash he's saved up over the years. I told him I'd ask you about it."

"Which one was it?" she said.

"Which guy? You know, I don't even know his name. Tall, thin guy, early eighties probably. I think he used to be an engineer of some kind. I've sat and talked to him a couple times when Pops would fall asleep on me, but I don't recall I ever asked his name."

"Well what makes him think that I would have any investment advice? I don't know anything about investments."

"I think he's looking to put it somewhere safe. In a bank or credit union, something like that. It's all in cash. Actual cash."

"How much cash is it?"

"Sweetie, I didn't inquire of the specifics, you know? But the way he talked, I got the feeling it was a lot. Like maybe his life savings or something. Apparently there are old people who do that. Lived through the depression, stock market collapse, and now they keep everything they have stuffed under a mattress."

"Except that now somebody else is changing his sheets," she said.

"Exactly."

"So he wants to put it in the bank now?"

"I don't know, I'm guessing. I do remember telling him about you and the girls, and I probably told him that you're a bank teller in town."

"We have to report any cash deposit over two thousand."

"Report to who?"

"There's this thing called the Suspicious Activity Report that goes to the federal government. I think that only applies to what it says, though. Money coming from a suspicious-looking person. But even if it's not suspicious, if it's more than ten thousand the person has to fill out a special IRS form. These days you can't even make a lot of small deposits. That will trigger a Suspicious Activity Report too."

"Interesting," I said. "A guy wants to put his own money into an account, where the bank can use it and make a profit from it, and the government has to investigate him."

"Yep. That's pretty much the way it works."

"So what should I tell the old guy next time I see him?"

"Personally? I'd tell him to spend it and enjoy himself. That's one thing you can still do with real money. Actually spend it."

"Spend it or give it away," I said.

"Hey. Maybe he'd like to buy me a new car."

"I'll mention that to him."

"Thanks," she said, and chuckled a little. "Tell him I like the color red."

*

So Cindy is sleeping finally, though I say finally only because every minute seems like an hour to me. She's always been able to say, "Goodnight, babe," and then roll over and go right out. Me, on the other hand, I've never been able to quiet my mind down that quickly, not even as a boy. Always had to play the entire day over in my head a few times, think about what I'd done wrong or should've done better. Up until I was fourteen or so the wrong things were usually stuff like letting a hard grounder sizzle past me, or bouncing a three-pointer off the rim. Though in high school it was all about girls, like how do I get her to notice me, did I say the right thing, should I put my hand on her breast or not. Then I enlisted and my worries were all about measuring up, not being the one who got chewed out in front of everybody. Once that fear passed I had a lot of other things to worry about, things that, when

I was a kid, I'd never even imagined. Everything from camel spiders to IEDs to freezing up and getting myself or somebody else killed.

You ever dream about those spiders, Spence? I sometimes dream those scary fuckers are chasing me. Man, could they run!

But anyway, I'm back home now. And none of the really bad shit I feared over there happened to me. So when it came to this thing I'd gotten myself into with the naked girl and the money, I figured if I kept at it and worked out all the angles, I could get myself out of that mess too. Only difference now is, I'm not in this mess alone. I'm a husband and a father. This is my squad and I'm responsible for their safety.

"Visualize your desired outcome," you always said. "Know your desired resolution for Plan A, Plan B. Know where the friendlies are. Know your exit strategy. Then pull up your panties, take a deep breath, and execute, motherfucker. Execute."

My situation is this: No police tape wrapped around the house on Route 218. No windows blacked out. No sign of a police raid. So, how to account for that? Two possibilities: Either the dispatcher who took my call is a friend of the druggies and gave them a heads-up, or, and this is the option that makes the most sense to me, the local police acted on my tip and visited the house, but found nothing to justify a search warrant. Which meant that the druggies cleaned everything up before the police arrived. And what would prompt them to do that? They came home, found muddy footprints all through their house, saw that a lot of their money was missing, and did a quick cleanup in anticipation of a possible visit from the po-po. Maybe the girl remembered me and maybe she didn't. Maybe somebody saw my bike and maybe not. In either case, the end result is the same: they know they've been ripped off.

Thing is, Spence, we knew some guys like that, didn't we? They were small-time, sure, what with the military eyeballing everything a soldier does. But, correct me if I'm wrong here, seems to me that every single one of them was a sneaky, hateful bastard pissed off at most of the world. So imagine if somebody made off with ninety thousand of their trust fund. What would they do to get it back? What wouldn't they do?

My Plan A, but only because it was the first plan to come to mind, was to return the money. Creep into the yard in the middle of the night, and as soon as that pit bull started barking, throw the shoebox onto the porch and run like hell. But have a vehicle parked not far down the road in case they turned the dog loose on me.

It sounded simple enough—undo the one thing I'd done wrong. But simple is never as simple as it looks. Would the druggies say, "Hey, isn't that nice? We got all our money back. Let's all go back to bed now."

Not likely. I pictured them being a good bit less forgiving than that. This is only a problem if they know who stole their money. And the only way they could know is if somebody recognized my bike.

Plan B is to do nothing. Don't spend any money, don't call attention to myself. Get busy looking for another job. Be the kind of man I want to be. Be the kind of husband and father Pops has always been.

That last part comes with obligations of its own. Should I tell Cindy about losing my job? Or should I save her the worry and wait until I have another job lined up?

I suspect I wouldn't have even been asking myself these questions if I didn't have all that money squirreled away. I'd probably have come home that day and told her all about my conversation with Jake, and both of us would have ranted awhile about the damn Chinese and how rotten a deal I was getting, and we'd both have been worried but not the way I am now. Because the truth of it is, a part of me wants to keep that money. A big part. Now that I have it, I want to keep it. Because now I really need it.

Man, all I ever wanted or expected out of life was to have a decent job for thirty years or so, stay reasonably healthy, raise good kids and put them on their own paths to success, and then enjoy my last twenty years or so playing with my grandkids. Don't want to be famous for anything, don't expect to be a millionaire. The only reality show people

I envy are the ones on *The Amazing Race*, but only because I think it would be so much fun for Cindy and me to go racing around the world together, seeing all the places and doing all the crazy things we're otherwise never going to experience.

More than once Cindy has said how she envies me getting to travel to the other side of the world. A lot more than once. Our little three-day honeymoon was the first time she'd ever even been out of the state. And the only time so far.

So lately I've been thinking something dangerous. This is Plan C; sort of my fantasy plan. What if I do have the money to take her someplace really special? What if I have the money to take the whole family there? Where would I take them?

There's this one guy I see on TV now and then when I'm channel surfing, and for some reason I always lay the remote down when I see him and listen for a while. He's not a preacher but he sounds like one, though without all the fake healing and hallelujahs. And the gist of his sermon is always the same thing: God wants us to be prosperous. He keeps putting opportunities for prosperity in front of us, but it's up to us to seize those opportunities. And I don't know, but I sit there and listen to him sometimes and I wonder, when am I going to get that opportunity?

And then there was this kid who worked washing dishes in the DFAC in Mahmudiya, an Egyptian boy named Musa something or other, you remember him? We all called him Moose. He was what, maybe fourteen or so, and he was always making deals everywhere he could, trading bootleg movies for porn DVDs, then trading the porn for a case of cheap Swadeshi whiskey that cost five bucks a bottle in Dahuk, then selling the whiskey to soldiers in Bagdad for five or six times as much. One of our own Bible thumpers would ask him, "What would Allah say about you cheating our new guys like that, Moose?" And Moose had two verses from the Koran he'd come back with: "Wealth and children are the ornament of this life." Or else this one: "Whatever the Apostle gives you, accept it; and whatever he forbids you, abstain from it."

So that night in bed with Cindy, while she's sleeping and I'm lying there awake trying to choose between Plans A, B and C, I have three advisors chattering in my head. I have that TV prosperity guy, I have Moose quoting the Koran, and I have Gee reminding me it's easier for a camel to pass through the eye of a needle than for a rich man to enter into the kingdom of Heaven.

And the only voice I try to argue with is Gee's.

*

The past few days have weighed on me like a sixty-pound rucksack, I swear. At night I can't sleep because of every little noise, and during the day at home I keep seeing shadows go past a window, which makes me jump up and start peeking outside, and of course there's nobody there. If a car follows me too long I pull over and let it go past and I check out the driver to see if he's going to pull over or, I don't know, do whatever a pissed-off druggie who's been robbed would do. I'm just paranoid as hell. Can't even stop to get gas without getting all twitchy if somebody looks my way.

Doesn't help being at work either. All we have to do at the plant is fill a couple of last orders, then start boxing up all the records and other documents. By Wednesday all the trucks were going out, with nothing coming in for processing. Jake spends a lot of time sitting at his desk and staring out the window at the piles of unprocessed rock.

I keep scanning the newspapers online and adding my name to any new job search engine I can find. I already posted my résumé online, so it gets shot off to any job I'm remotely qualified for. Financial Analyst I, Supply Chain Specialist, Accounts Receivable Processor, Purchasing Manager, Quality Control . . .

And, just like the week before, nobody calls me for an interview. Either my business administration degree from a nowhere college is worthless, or I'm putting out so much negative energy that my résumé reeks of failure.

And after feeling like a worthless human being all day, I have to walk back into my house with a phony smile on my face.

Thursday night, Dani complained that her throat hurt. Cindy checked her temperature, 101.6. We gave her a dose of Children's Tylenol and put her to bed. In our own bedroom a few minutes later, Cindy said, "If she's not better in the morning, I'm going to take her to the doctor. Her tonsils look inflamed to me. It's probably time she had them taken out."

I didn't answer because I couldn't. My heart was beating like a wild duck in that moment it explodes off the water, trying like crazy to get airborne. Because all I could think about was that our medical coverage will end in a few days. After that, the first time Cindy hands our medical card to a pharmacist or the doctor's secretary, she's going to find out how I let the family down. She'll see me in all my naked deception and failure. I don't think I have any option but to tell her about my job. Not that telling her will change anything. The only thing it might accomplish is to preserve my integrity. That little bit of it I still have left.

Anyway, come morning, Dani's forehead was hotter than ever, and when she swallowed some more of the medicine she moaned and screwed up her mouth. I saw that look in Cindy's face that told me she was going to start worrying at double speed now, going to let every little worry bang through her like a train going off its tracks.

"Tell you what," I said. "You get ready for work. I'll get the girls dressed and after we drop you at the bank we'll drive over to the Med Express. If the doctor won't clear Dani for daycare, and he probably won't, I'll bring the girls back home and play dolls with them all day."

"Jake will let you do that?" she asked.

I thought about telling her then. But I couldn't. I don't know why; I just couldn't.

"We're between orders," I told her. "Days when that happens, we sit around and look at each other. I'll go in for a while tomorrow to do the end-of-week reports."

Two hours later I'm building a tent with blankets in the living room. I let the girls get back into their pj's so they can spend the day in the tent, watching cartoons out through the front flap. I stay in there with them for an hour or so, but I keep catching myself looking at Dani every couple of minutes and thinking, get better fast, please get better fast. Dr. Sherry at the Med Express said she was going to call the hospital and see when they could schedule Dani for a tonsillectomy, and she'd let us know but to expect mid-September sometime. I said, "Can't she have them taken out now? Like, today?" But she had to do a ten-day treatment of antibiotics first. My insurance would run out before the meds did. So all morning long my body's feeling like it's on fire inside, because my own train of worries has not only run off its tracks but careened over a mountainside and is crashing, car over car, toward the bottom.

It's funny how when bad things start happening in a series, it almost seems as if they're all related somehow, as if each one is causing the next. I remember you talking about that one time, about what you called your Domino Catastrophe Theory. You said the universe is filled to the brim with bad things waiting to happen, not only the universe of everything but also each one of our own personal universes too. "There's a 50–50 chance that one fuckup, no matter how small, is going to trigger another one," you said. "And if that happens, there's a 70–30 chance that the second one will trigger a total clusterfuck."

Remember Hetrick? He always struck me as a fairly pleasant guy except that he wouldn't believe anything he hadn't personally experienced. If you told him the sky is blue, he'd look up and check it out before he'd tell you, "I guess it is."

I remember him saying, after you told us about your Catastrophe Theory, "Well, if that's true, then by now life would be nothing but one continuous Charlie Foxtrot."

"Which it is, to an extent," you told him. "But bear in mind that every individual fuckup requires energy, negative energy. And every once in a while the energy dissipates to the point that there's a nice little lull in the action. Plus," you said, "there's always a degree of uncertainty about how energy and time will react with one another. Then throw into that uncertainty the person or persons involved in the fuckup, and the degree of unpredictability escalates beyond any degree of certainty whatsoever."

Hey, I can almost hear you laughing right now. Can hear you asking me, "You actually remember all that bullshit?" It's funny but I do. I think I've always known I'm not one of the sharpest tools in the shed, which is why I always pay special attention when somebody smarter than me has something to say. And you—I always idolized you in a way. One tour under your belt already, those three stripes on your sleeve. Plus that way you had of never getting rattled, that was the most amazing thing of all to me.

Anyway, back to your Catastrophe Theory. Most of us were laughing our asses off, because if there was any sense to what you were saying, it was sailing away about six feet over our heads. Only Hetrick was taking it seriously. "There's a name for that kind of thinking," he said. "It's called total bullshit."

"Actually," you told him, never even cracking a smile, "it's called quantum physics. If you spent a little more time reading, and a lot less time pounding your pud over that cheerleader back in Hickory who has probably sucked off the entire football team by now, you might actually learn a little something about how reality works. There's a lot more to it than an illiterate hillbilly who is only good at converting oxygen to carbon dioxide can even imagine."

I remember feeling a little bit sorry for Hetrick after that, because he did seem to have a fairly limited outlook on life. Personally, I was always interested in your ideas, even when I didn't understand them. I mean I listened hard to everything you told us, not only because you were my Squad Leader and had a lot more experience than the rest of us, but also because, let's face it, you were obviously a lot smarter than all of us put together. The first time I heard you talk, I thought to myself, pay attention to this guy, and maybe you can learn a thing or two.

And son of a gun if most of the things you said back then haven't begun to make more sense to me. Your Catastrophe Theory, for example. I know that logically it makes no sense to think that the Chinese buying out the plant and making my job evaporate had anything to do with me stopping to help that girl, but actually it does. I wouldn't even have seen that girl if I hadn't been so upset that I jumped on my bike without putting on my rain gear first, and if I had put on my rain gear I wouldn't have been so impatient to get out of the rain, and I wouldn't have taken the back way home. And that led to me taking the money. And who's to say that my worry and negative energy over taking it didn't somehow cause Dani's strep throat and even attract Cindy's father, Mr. Negative Energy Himself, back into her life?

If I wanted to I could even take the string of causes back even further, and tie in all the little things that did or didn't happen before I carried that naked girl into her house. If my memory was good enough, I could probably take it all the way back through my mother's tumble down the basement stairs and before that to the man who shot his seed into her and then was never heard from again.

Gee would probably say you could take it all the way back to that apple in the Garden of Eden if you wanted to. And you would probably have said, Why stop there? Why not take it back to the darkness and the void, back to Genesis verse 1. That's the place to look for answers, you would say. That's the place to stand there in the nothingness and scream at the top of your lungs, *What the hell were you thinking?*

*

Spending the morning alone with my girls, something I seldom get a chance to do, it was tough to keep my mind off the money. Truth is, it was impossible to keep my mind off the money. I'd watch little Emma in there in our blanket tent pretending to see polar bears and Indians out in the living room, or I'd listen to Dani pretending we were on the *Survivorman* TV show and having to roast lizards and bats over the fire for dinner, and how could I not think to myself how great it would be if I had the money to take them on a real camping trip somewhere? Take them out West, for example, and let them gawk at the Grand Canyon and bug out their little eyes at the sight of a real mountain or an elk or a herd of wild horses?

And then I would think, you do have the money, stupid. You have the money to take them anywhere you want.

And then I'd push that thought aside for a while. But sooner or later, it always came slinking back, whispering its poison.

*

I was half-asleep on the couch, and the girls were asleep in the tent, when I heard what sounded like a thump at the back door. The only people who use the back door are a couple of neighbors. Cindy and the girls and me do the same thing when we go to their houses, I'm not sure why. It seems less formal, I guess, than to knock at their front doors the way a stranger would.

So there's this loud knock on the back door, and I sit up with a jerk, and of course, as paranoid as I am, my first thought is that it's the druggies coming to get their money back. I don't even know who they are, what they look like, how many of them there are, nothing. But I freeze, man. I just sit there like a deer in the headlights.

Then there's a second knock, even louder, and I get up and go creeping out into the kitchen, thinking I'll take a quick peek out the pantry door and if I don't like what I see I'll make a mad dash to the garage and grab the revolver from my saddlebag. I mean I'm ready to do it. I've got two little girls asleep in their tent. I'll do whatever I have to do.

But a glance out the glass in the pantry door is all I need. It's Janice standing out there, Cindy's mother. Donnie's standing behind Janice and smoking a cigarette, looking fairly pleased with himself, like he sold some schmuck a used car for twice its actual value. Janice is smiling too, but with a lot less conviction than Donnie. She's wearing way too much makeup, but not enough to hide that sort of dazed and rumpled look she always has. Pops would say she looks like she's been rode hard and put away wet.

I open the door a crack and say to Donnie, "You want to blow that smoke away from the door?"

Janice turns to him and says, "Put it out, Donnie, okay?" He gives me a big grin, sucks in another lungful, drops the butt down to the cement slab and grinds it out with his foot. Then he turns away from me and blows the smoke out his mouth.

Janice says, "We came to check on the girls, honey. How are my babies doing?"

"They're sleeping right now," I tell her. "Did Cindy call you?"

"We thought you could maybe use a hand with the girls."

It didn't sound at all like Cindy to ask her mother to come help me out. I'd called her after we left the doctor's office, told her about the tonsillectomy in our future, but it was a short conversation because she was working behind her teller's window. About an hour after that I got a text from her that said, *You need anything? Dani okay?* And I texted back, *Everything fine. Going camping in the living room.*

And then it hit me. Janice is one of those people who goes to the doctor twice a week or so to get whatever kind of prescription she can wangle. I'm fairly certain she patronizes a couple of different doctors and a couple of different pharmacies. Today was probably her day for the Med Express.

I told her, "We're good, thanks. I'd rather not disturb their nap."

"Can't we come in and take a peek at them? It's been a long time since Donnie's even seen them."

"I bet they've grown like weeds," he said.

I didn't give him any reaction, didn't even turn my eyes to him. To Janice I say, "Can I talk to you a minute?" And I hold the door open just enough that she can squeeze inside. The second she's over the threshold I close the door behind her.

"What's wrong, honey?" she says.

"Look. Cindy doesn't want him anywhere near this place. She told me that straight out."

She clicked her tongue. "I wish I knew what in the world she has against him. He's her father, for God's sake."

I said nothing to that, so she looked up at me and asked, "Why is she so mad at him all the time?"

"You'd know that better than me," I said.

She scowled and shook her head, as if the whole situation was beyond her comprehension. "He used to be overly critical sometimes, I know. But he's not that way anymore."

"I think maybe the problem was bigger than that."

"There's nothing else to it," she said. "She makes things up, is all. She always has."

"I've never known her to make anything up."

"Well she's going to have to get used to this situation. He's going to be around now. He's part of the family."

"Janice," I told her. "Let me put it to you this way. You're always welcome here. But if he so much as ever sets foot inside this house again, I'm going to punch him in the face."

That was probably the first time all morning her eyes came all the way open. Then she blinked at me a couple times. I sort of felt bad when she started to tear up, because I'm not usually the kind of guy who says things so bluntly. But then she turned away and jerked open the door and stepped out to him, giving him just enough time to look at me with a hurt and puzzled expression on his face before she took him by the arm and yanked him around.

*

That evening, my camping buddies and me picked up Cindy at the bank. I could tell by the way she came striding across the parking lot that she was seriously ticked off about something. She glared at me when she climbed in, then turned off the look long enough to smile at the girls in the seat behind us and ask, "My baby girls doing okay?" After she talked to the girls a minute or two, she hit me with that glare again.

"So how was your day?" I asked her as I was pulling out into the traffic.

"I need to stop at the store and get some Jell-O," she said.

"I think there's a couple boxes in the cupboard," I told her.

"You think so or you know so?"

I figured she was either pissed at me for threatening to punch her father, or because she found out that the plant was closing. The first option seemed highly unlikely. She was more likely to be pissed because I didn't punch him. Which left the second option.

For the rest of the ride home I kept my mouth shut and did what I was told.

Back at the house, she got the girls settled in front of the TV with a couple of pudding cups, then she said to me, "I want to talk to you in the garage."

I wasn't even down off the garage steps before she spun around and said, "Did you think I would never find out?"

I froze for a second or two, long enough for a feeling of cold dread to wash over me. Then I said, "Who'd you hear it from?"

"Well apparently everybody in town knows about it except me. Apparently I'm the last person to find out. You know what I heard at least a half-dozen times today? *You mean Russell didn't tell you? I can't believe Russell never told you about it!* Do you know how embarrassing that is?"

You know that sick, gut-punched feeling you get when you let down somebody you love? That's what I was feeling. "Sweetie," I told her, "I'm sorry. I wanted to find another job before I told you. I didn't want you to worry about it."

"Well I am worried. I'm very worried. We're going to have another baby in March!"

Because she wasn't showing yet, it was easy at times to forget she was pregnant. Easy for me, I mean. I doubt I'd ever stop thinking about a baby if there was one inside me.

"How much longer before you're done?" Cindy asked.

It takes me a while to say it, but I know I have to. "It would have been today. But now it's tomorrow."

"Dani needs a tonsillectomy! How are we going to pay for that without insurance? Plus there's the mortgage, the truck payment, the . . . the . . ."

I grabbed her and pulled her close and told her, *"Shhhh, shhhh,"* while I stroked her hair. "I'll find a job, I promise. If I have to I'll get on with Burger King or Mickey D's. Those places are always looking for managers."

"You didn't go to college to manage a bunch of teenagers," she said.

"I went to college to get a degree so I could take care of my family. And that's what I'll do. However I have to."

"It's not the long term I'm worried about," she said. "You'll find a job, probably even a better one. But even if it only takes you till Thanksgiving, that's three months we have to get through on my income alone. We can't make our payments on that!"

"There's some stuff of Pops' I can use," I told her.

80

"What stuff?"

"Stuff I stored for him. He says it's mine anytime I want it. Old coins, silver certificates . . . It's probably worth a few thousand anyway. Enough to keep our heads above water for a while."

"Are you sure it's safe out there?" she said.

"Pops and I are the only ones who know it's there."

"Is he still going to give us his car? We could probably sell that for a couple thousand."

"I'm pretty sure he wants to keep it until they take his license from him."

Then she started crying again. "We don't even have any college funds started. We need to have three of them."

"Ah, baby," I said, and I pulled her close again, although I needed it as much as she did. "I'll ask Jake if he knows anybody who might take me on. I'll get us a paycheck somehow. You know I will."

She nodded and sniffed a little. "Maybe you'd better get those things out of storage and bring them here. We need to figure out what we have to work with."

"I will," I said.

She sniffed again, then patted her hand against my chest a couple of times. "I need to get to work on dinner."

"Why don't you let me do it."

"I need to keep busy."

"I'll do some hot dogs on the grill, you make a fruit salad."

"Dani needs something easy to swallow. Tomato soup okay?"

"With grilled cheese? Sure."

She nodded and pulled away a couple of inches, but she didn't let go of me yet. "I didn't mean to sound angry," she said. "I mean I was but . . . mostly I'm just scared to death."

"You don't have to be," I told her. "Worse comes to worst, I can always go back in the Army."

"Oh no you don't," she said. "This is our home. You're not leaving it again and neither are we."

"All right, boss," I told her. "I'm here to stay."

*

You probably think I'm taking a long time getting around to the important stuff, don't you? Thing is, every time I sit down here in the middle of the night and start typing, I remember more. And it all seems important to me. Sometimes I even get a little bit lost in remembering. But that's not really a bad thing, is it?

Anyway, to get back to where I left off last time. That night in bed, I felt a strange tension between Cindy and me. I thought at first it was all coming from me, because there were things I still hadn't told her and couldn't figure out whether to or not. And I only felt worse about it when she started touching me, letting me know she wanted to make love. It was the kind of touching she does when she is sad or worried, face-touching I call it, as opposed to the kind when she wants sex and goes straight for the lower hemisphere. The face-touching starts out with nuzzling, and with her fingertips tracing all the contours of my face as if she's blind and can only see me by touch. It took me a couple of years with her to realize what that kind of touching means, but once I did, I always found it a lot more arousing than her more direct approach, and I would get hard in an instant.

The face-touching meant she wanted me to take charge but in a slow, gentle way, taking my time and giving some close attention to her own face, her lips and ears and neck, light touches and kisses part by part until I would gradually slide down with the lower half of my body hanging off the foot of the bed. These were the only times she liked me to do that to her, which also accounts for why I would typically get hard the moment I saw what kind of night it was going to be.

Usually nights like that were a kind of torture for me, but crazy good at the same time. On those nights she required a lot of slow attention to get where she wanted to be, while all the time I'm like a trigger that's one millimeter from being tripped. Sometimes I would even have to distract myself to keep my body in check, so I would keep reminding myself, no sudden movements, boy. I couldn't even touch myself for fear of going off like a firecracker, at least not until I'd feel the ripples start on the inside of her thigh.

That moment was always one of the most arousing things for me. Her hands on the top of my head would tell me to keep doing what I was doing, and then she would grab two fistfuls of hair and pull on me and say "Now baby, now baby," and I would slide up on top of her and inside her and suddenly both of us would be tumbling like meteors down through the sweetest, deepest darkness we'd ever felt.

It makes me a little uncomfortable to talk about this part of our life, but you were always the only one I could talk about it with, Spence. And it never seemed to make you the least bit uncomfortable then, so I'm sure it doesn't now either. I only bring it up because of how different it was for us that night after she found out I was losing my job.

I did everything that night I usually do, but it wasn't getting her anywhere. So after a while she kind of sighed and said, "That's enough, baby." And immediately everything in me went flat too. Getting her off is as enjoyable for me as getting myself off, and I always felt guilty if I came and she didn't. She wanted to take care of me, of course, and she slipped her hand between my legs to get started. But then she pulled back and said, "You too?"

"I guess we're both too tense tonight," I told her.

"Just hold me then. Sometimes that's the best thing anyway."

So I held her and kept trying to come up with a single good reason to tell her about the money. But the only reason I could find was that we were married and had agreed to always be 100 percent honest with each other. Still, that reason didn't seem to outweigh the consequences of involving her in the stupid decision I'd made.

In the end I tried to make myself feel a little better by bringing up the other bit of news.

"Did you talk to your mother today?" I asked.

"No. Why?"

"You didn't call her while you were at work?"

"I haven't talked to her in three or four days."

"She came by the house today."

"She did? When was this?"

"Somewhere around two o'clock, I guess."

"What did she want?"

"She said she came to see how Dani was doing. Apparently she knew about the sore throat, knew that we were home for the day."

She pulled away from me and half sat up. "How would she know that?"

"All I can figure is that she talked to Dr. Sherry today."

"Oh. Yeah, probably. Though there's that one receptionist who works there . . ."

"Toni? The one with red hair. That's who was there today."

"Toni, yeah. I think they used to hang out together. Maybe still do."

"Okay, then. Mystery solved."

She laid back down beside me then, but only for a few seconds. "The girls didn't say a word about seeing her today."

"They were asleep in the tent."

"The whole time?"

I blew out a breath. "She brought your father along. I wouldn't let him into the house. So your mother didn't stay all that long."

"Oh God," she said. "Damn her! Damn damn damn damn damn—"

I rolled up close and held her face against my chest, telling her *"Shhh, shhh,"* until she quieted down and lay still. But her stillness was as hard as stone, so I kept my arms around her and bundled her up against me.

It was maybe ten minutes or so before the anger drained out of her and she started sobbing. I kept doing what I was doing, which was the only thing I knew to do. And when she stopped sobbing there wasn't anything left in her but a hoarse and miserable sadness that broke my heart in two.

"Everything is falling apart for us," she said.

I said, "No it's not, baby. I will never let that happen."

"You promise?" she said. "Will you promise me that?"

"I swear to God," I told her. But there are different ways of swearing, aren't there, Spence? And I didn't tell her which one I was using.

Next morning I crawled out of bed with a good idea of how it feels to be a zombie. I hadn't had a decent night's sleep all week. It was another nice day outside, but neither the sunshine nor the bike ride to work chased my cobwebs away, so I pulled in at the convenience store a few minutes from the plant. First thing I did was to gas up, then I left my bike at the pump and went inside and filled the biggest cup available with the blackest coffee available. I knew I'd have to drink at least half of it before attempting to ride to work with the cup tucked into my crotch, so I'm standing there sipping through the lid hole when I noticed a pretty girl coming through the door. And I guess I did what all guys do when they see a pretty girl, I checked her out.

But only for maybe three seconds total. That's all I needed. Because even with clothes on, she was impossible to not recognize.

She went straight to the doughnut case and started filling up a box. Suddenly I didn't need the coffee anymore, so I set it down beside the coffee pots and headed outside without paying. I passed within a foot of her on my way to the door, plenty close enough to see the yellowing bruise under her right eye and to notice the way her hand was shaking as she worked the tongs under a doughnut.

You know that state of being hyperalert you used to talk about? That's where I was all of a sudden, moving in what felt like slow motion toward the door, keeping myself out of her peripheral vision while seeing every detail of her as I passed. You said there's a knowledge that comes from being in that state when all the details of observation come together, and that it's important to trust that flash of knowledge because it's almost always true. Well, I can tell you without a glimmer of doubt, Spence, that I knew somebody had kicked the shit out of that girl. I knew with an absolute and awful certainty that she had been going through hell ever since that rainy day I first saw her, same as I had, except that hers was a physical hell and mine was a mental one.

More importantly, I knew why.

I'll tell you the truth, brother. If I'd had the money on me at that particular moment, and if I'd known which vehicle was hers, I would have dumped the money in her front seat and hightailed it out of there while she was still picking out her doughnuts. That might have stopped the dominoes in your catastrophe theory from banging into each other.

But I didn't have the money with me. And the dominoes didn't stop falling.

*

After seeing that girl at the doughnut case, I pulled into work so out of breath and confused I didn't even notice the SUV until I walked right up to it. I parked my bike behind the office same as always, not far from Jake's pickup truck, but the SUV didn't really register on me until I started walking toward the office door. And that's when it hit me. I turned around and looked straight at the shiny black vehicle and I even said out loud what I was thinking. "The fucking Chinese are here."

Up until that realization sort of poleaxed me, I'd been trying to figure out how to get in touch with you. I felt like I was stumbling around blindly, like I had my goggles on but they were caked with sand and the wind was blasting so hard against me that I was losing ground moving backward. I needed somebody to talk to and you were the only likely candidate. I wasn't ready to bring either Pops or Cindy into this mess, and you were the only other levelheaded guy I'd ever been close to. You always had an answer, Spence, even if it was only something like, stand still, nimrod, and think! Which way were you headed? Which direction is the wind blowing? One plus one equals the way back to camp. So stand here a minute and use the brain God gave you.

Still, it had been almost six years since I'd seen you, and those couple of e-mails we exchanged after I was back home was the last I knew of your whereabouts. The last one from you said you were headed to SFAS at Mackall and that you'd be hard to reach for a couple of months. Then a good while later I had one from Rainey telling me about the hell you guys went through in Korengal, and how he was back home now and had lost touch with you too. I thought I could probably track you down though, and even if all we talked about was the weather, maybe that would be enough to quiet the sandstorm raging in my head.

But then there was that SUV all of a sudden, so shiny black in the morning light. Up until then I'd never noticed how quiet and clear the air could be when the crushers and separator are shut down. Everything was absolutely motionless all of a sudden, except that I was so furious I wanted to take a sledgehammer to that vehicle. I wanted to break out every inch of glass and beat that black metal into the ground.

Silly, I know. Absolutely useless.

I go into the office and there's Jake sitting at his desk and staring out the window same as always. I don't even bother to sit down. "Any reason I need to be here today?" I ask him. "What I really need to be doing is looking for a job."

It takes him fifteen seconds or so to turn his head my way. "I was thinking of leaving myself," he says. "It's eating me up to see this finally happening."

"So let's both leave," I tell him, and now I'm thinking maybe I can talk about the girl and the money with him, maybe he'll have an idea or two I can use.

"One of us has to hang around in case they have any questions," he says. "You know the operation as well as I do."

"I've been here half a year, Jake. You've got forty years in. You built this place."

"You don't have to do anything," he tells me. "You can look for jobs on the computer, can't you? Make phone calls. All I'm asking is that you hang out here until they leave."

I blow out a breath. "You're still the boss," I say.

He stands up, pats his pockets, finds his key ring in the letter tray. "Do me a favor and don't answer the phone if it rings," he says. "The newspaper called first thing this morning."

"What'd you tell them?"

"I hung up. That's why they keep calling back."

"You got to talk to them sometime, don't you?"

"I don't owe them anything. Let them talk to the Chinese if they want a story so bad. Damned if I'll volunteer to be their whipping boy."

Three minutes later, I'm standing there alone.

It's probably another hour before I actually see them. Four guys in what look like gray lab coats and white hard hats. My stomach's churning, and there's hot, sour bile rising up in my throat. They're out at the edge of the property line, standing beside a surveyor's stake and looking in toward the building, talking and nodding to one another. I grab my own hard hat off the top of the filing cabinet and go on out to where they are.

They stand there smiling while I walk up to them and tell them good morning. One guy is holding a camera, another has a clipboard. They give me four little head bows, and I don't know whether to bow in return or not. I really don't know what to do or exactly why I walked out to them.

I tell them my name and that I'm the foreman, or used to be anyway, and I ask if they have any questions, if there's anything I can tell them about the operation. One of the two who isn't carrying anything translates for the other ones. He speaks better English than I do except for what sounds to me like a British accent. Then a guy with short gray hair visible under his hard hat says maybe five words in Chinese. Then the one who speaks English thanks me and says they have everything under control. The demolition will begin in two weeks, he says. Then all new equipment will arrive, dust control, noise suppression, everything state of the art. He says they'll be filling orders again before Day of Thanksgiving in America. That's what he calls it, Day of Thanksgiving in America. They're all beaming at me like happy babies and I'm trying to smile but my mouth feels stiff and crooked and I am 90 percent certain I am going to throw up.

"So what are the chances," I finally say, "of you gentlemen keeping me on in some capacity? I don't have to be foreman or anything. I understand all the equipment. I can even drive a truck if you need somebody for that."

This time the translator doesn't even bother to translate. Doesn't even bother to answer me. I get a nod and a smile. Four smiles all in a row. I wonder if I'm expected to bow or something, but I can't make myself do it, and so finally I turn around and walk away. I go back to the office and pull the blinds down and put in my eight hours and then leave.

Instead of going home, though, I ride out to Pops' storage unit and sit in the darkness with the door pulled down. All day long I've been feeling like my brain is swollen inside my skull, like the pressure in there is going to split my head wide open. I felt that same thing during the last weeks of my rotation in Iraq, but there was no quiet place there where a guy could spend some time alone, so I dealt with it by pushing myself through all the drills and exercises. Coming back to the FOB after a patrol was the worst time of all. You'd think a guy would feel grateful to make it back to his cot in one piece, but as every soldier knows, you lay there with your body depleted and your brain so wired you have no choice but to replay every move that day, every doorway that might be hiding somebody in its shadows, every bit of trash that might have an IED hidden under it. You keep going over and over and over it all again until some part of your brain finally gets the message that it's okay to let go for a while, and that you had better let go and catch some zzz's because you're going to be outside the wire again in a few hours.

Even after I was discharged I wasn't able to let go completely. People congratulating me and saying how lucky I was to come home without a scratch, and me with a wife and two little girls and not enough smarts to even know how to spell résumé, let alone write one. There wasn't much call back home here for a guy who could field strip an M4 in the dark and make it through day after day of hundred-degree heat in full battle rattle. The Army gave me just enough training to realize how useless I was back home.

That first year in college, Spence, was rougher than Basic. I'd sit there in a classroom surrounded by kids who thought life was a reality TV show and they were all auditioning for the lead role. I hated every one of them. And I'm not saying it was their fault I hated them, it was mine. I was jealous because their Nike shoes and Hollister hoodies and Calvin Klein jeans cost more than I took home working campus security sixty hours a month. But the real reason I hated them was because I had something they didn't and never would, which was a head full of little bits of days and nights when I was sure I was going to die.

I made it through college too, though. I had no choice but to get the job done. I never told Cindy about the nightmares that would wake me up at night, never told her I would slip out of bed at two or three in the morning to go sit in the living room with the TV on without any sound. She knew, though. And sometimes she'd just look at me afterward like I was something pathetic, like a dog dying by the side of the road after it's been hit by a car.

I never told her how much I wanted a few days off without any kind of obligation to fulfill, a couple days to myself in a cabin in the woods, or even a tent pitched beside a stream somewhere. Some quiet place to detox all on my own, you know? A place to bleed it all out if I could.

Having Jake take me on was pretty close to being the best day of my life. Holding Dani and Emma for the first time, those were the very best, but knowing I'd learned a little something in college and had a job and could take care of my family, that put the nightmares to rest for a while.

I always half expected I was going to fuck up in a major way in Iraq and get myself or lots of other people killed. Then I expected to make an ass of myself in college somehow, and I guess I avoided that by keeping my mouth shut most of the time. What I never once expected was that helping some girl too doped up to keep her clothes on was going to be what did me in.

A lot of people probably wouldn't understand why I was so messed up about stealing money from a drug dealer. I mean I know all their arguments, I make them to myself a few times every day. Stealing from a drug dealer isn't stealing, they would say. Take it and enjoy it. Put it to good use. Be happy you got away with it.

Thing is, I didn't feel like I had gotten away with anything. First off, Pops and Gee didn't raise me to be the kind of person who would steal from anybody. They raised me to be responsible, and to always do what was right. I always did my best to give them what they wanted. Then I gave the Army what it wanted. Then I gave my professors what they wanted. And all along the way I gave Cindy and the girls what they wanted from me.

I made little mistakes, sure. A few too many beers when I was underage, a bit of weed here and there. But if I did anything wrong, I only did it to myself. Stealing that money, though, involved my entire family in one way or another. Secrets and lies always do that, always have a way of snowballing. And now, seeing that girl at the convenience store that morning, it hit me hard, knowing that she was getting knocked around because of something I did.

And there's another reason too, Spence, that I felt so bad after seeing her again. You don't know how close I came to doing what she wanted to do that day. Truth is, I probably would have let her blow me if I hadn't seen those boxes in the shower stall. She was messed up but she was beautiful. Plus I was soaking wet and cold and I'd lost my job and felt like a worthless piece of shit. I could have used a little favor. I felt rotten knowing I was probably going to let her do it, but I wanted it, I really did. And then I saw the money.

So when I add up all the ways I'd become less than the man I wanted to be, all the ways I'd brought trouble into the lives of other people . . .

Spence, I sat there in the darkness of Pops' storage unit with his revolver in my hand and a small fortune at my back. And I thought of how ashamed of me you would be if I did what I was thinking of doing. I thought about you and the rest of the company up on top of that naked hill overlooking the Korengal, taking fire from three directions for most of seventy-two hours because the idiots in charge had issued metal detectors that never made a beep over the plastic mines. I thought about Rainey with his leg blown off, and how he'd always thought he could man-muscle his way through a stone wall if he had to. I thought about you guys hunkered down there in the holes you dug, same as me hunkered down in Pops' storage unit, and I could picture you, Spence, running around like a crazy mother hen during those long hours, checking on all your chicks, calling out their names again and again and again while you waited for the sound of choppers or missiles or anything else the gods out in the sandbox decided to send.

And I thought about Cindy and me growing up without fathers, and I knew what that would be like for my own girls. I didn't want that for them. I wanted them to have all the opportunities and all the nice things Cindy and me never got.

And the only way I could accomplish that was to get hard again. I had to stop beating myself up over things I couldn't change. I had to man up and do whatever ugly things I might be called upon to do.

*

I wish like hell I could stop thinking about that naked girl. I keep imagining her sucking my dick, and about fucking her on that bare mattress in the meth house. And it's hard, angry fucking. There's nothing sweet about it. I even jerk off thinking about her. Then afterward I feel like whale shit, the lowest of the low.

For a while back there in the sandbox I used to jerk off to that other girl, the one you kept Perry from raping. What I never told you about that incident, what I was always too ashamed to tell you, was that before you came into that room and stopped him, I'd been there from the very beginning. I was there when he grabbed her and dragged her into the room, I was there when he ripped off her clothes and pushed her down onto the floor. I was standing there staring at her breasts and her bush and doing nothing to help her. Not so much as a word to tell him to stop.

Then all of a sudden there you are pushing past me and grabbing him and yanking him around just as he's about to let his pants fall to the floor. You're screaming, "What the fuck do you think you're doing, soldier!" and he's whipping out his Beretta and bringing it up toward your face and that's when I finally came unfrozen and smacked the M4's butt into his chest.

Afterward I told you I'd stepped into the room only a nanosecond before you did. I was pretty sure you knew I was lying, but you never once challenged me on it. And I hated myself for that. Both for lying to you and for thinking what I'd been thinking before you showed up.

What makes us act like such animals sometimes, Spence? I don't want to be an animal. I want to be a man. I want to be a good husband and father and somebody who doesn't flinch when he looks at himself in the mirror.

Jesus, Spence. What am I supposed to do with all this crazy shit?

*

That night after talking to the Chinese, and then hunkering down for a while in Pops' storage unit, and finding my balls, I guess you'd say, I swung by the mall on the way and returned home carrying an armload of books. Why I chose books, I'm not really sure. But I'd been thinking about the times I loved best in all my life, and they were always the quiet times, you know? With the girls, it was when I read to them at night, the three of us crowded onto Dani's bed, Emma with her head in my lap and me reaching over her to hold Dani's hand while I held the book in my other hand, and the way the girls smelled after their baths, and Emma's little mouth when she fell asleep making that *shhh, shhh* sound against my pant leg.

And with Cindy it was those weekend afternoons when she was pregnant with Dani. She was supposed to stay in bed as much as possible, so I wore out my shoes going back and forth to the library for her. And I remembered how her eyes would light up when I'd come home and dump a load of books down beside her, and then she'd grab one and start reading out loud, and most times I'd fall asleep there lying up against her, the same way the girls do with me, and I'd be thinking as I drifted off how peaceful and sweet our lives together had become.

Anyway, I went home that night with books for everybody. Picture books for Emma and Easy Readers for Dani and a couple of Lemony Snicket books for me to read to them. For Cindy I got a boxed set of paperbacks. We had watched all of those movies about the girl who loves a vampire and a werewolf, and after every one we had the same friendly argument, with me saying how stupid it was to choose a white-skinned soulless dude over a hunky werewolf, and Cindy saying that the pale guy was so tragic and damned that of course the girl would love him better.

Dani and Emma squealed and hugged me when they saw the books, and at first Cindy's eyes lit up like they used to but then they went dark again and she stood there looking at me until the girls went running off to the living room with their presents.

I said, "You can exchange them if you want to. I know we already saw the movies, so you know how everything ends. I didn't know what else you might like."

"It's not that," she said. "Today was your last day of work. We don't have any idea how we're going to pay our bills, and you spend what, a hundred dollars or more on books?"

"Baby, a hundred dollars isn't going to make any difference one way or the other."

"A hundred dollars is four bags of groceries," she said.

"I wanted to do something to cheer you up is all."

"It's not that I don't appreciate it," she said.

"But it doesn't cheer you up, does it?"

"We can't eat books, Russell. We can't pay a doctor's bill with books."

I never intended to show her the rest I'd brought home, but at the time it seemed like I should. "I forgot something," I said, and then I went back to the garage and then back to her carrying a wad of twenties and fifties in my hand. I laid it on the table beside her empty plate. She just stood there staring at it, and then after a while she looked up and stared at me.

"That's my termination bonus," I told her. "It was a thousand dollars until I bought the books."

"Really?" she said, and then the tears came into her eyes and she started crying and I stepped up and put my arms around her and held her tight against me.

"I'm sorry I'm so afraid," she said, and she was shivering in my arms. "I know you'll do anything to take care of us. I know you will."

I stroked her hair and held her, and when she was ready she pulled away and scooped up the money and stuffed it into the rooster cookie jar with the money she had been saving for Dani's school lunches and such. Then she went to the oven and looked in at the tuna noodle casserole she'd made.

"Can you tell the girls to go wash their hands?" she said. Then, a second later, "Wait. Did you know you were getting that bonus?"

"Didn't have a clue," I told her.

That night I read for a half hour to the girls, and when I went into our bedroom Cindy was sitting there in bed reading the first book from her set. I showered and brushed and then slid in beside her. She reached out and squeezed my hand but kept right on reading.

"Read to me," I said, and she said, "Really?"

"Like you used to," I told her. "I miss that."

I didn't care about the words but only the sound of her voice, the way it reminded me of Gee and my mom when I was little. And after a while I had to turn my face to the wall, but I couldn't bear to let go of her hand.

*

What happened to the next day, Sunday, I can't really say. It's pretty much gone from my memory. A guy loses his job and it's like, Who am I now? What's my definition now? Sure, I'm still a father and husband, but part of that definition, a big part, is being a good provider for the family. Losing your job, even when you know it's coming, is like suddenly having your legs cut off.

I guess I went through all the motions that day with my head in a fog, not really knowing who I was or what I was going to do next or how I was going to get that part of my definition back. Especially now that another definition, one I never wanted, the one called thief, was sucking all the energy from me. I mean literally sucking me dry.

*

The next morning I woke up gasping for air, though I didn't know why. Couldn't remember if I'd been having a bad dream or not. But I woke up in a panic with my heart racing a mile a minute, beating hard against my chest, thumping in my temples the way it used to when we were moving door to door against those mud walls. It was the open doorways that scared me the most, the ones that didn't have to be yanked open before a gun barrel would show itself. A man could stand in those shadows and never be seen, not a ripple of movement until you saw the muzzle flash itself, by which time it's already way too late.

Anyway, that's how I woke up Monday morning, out of breath, heart beating like an old generator in those last two seconds before it runs out of gas, like it knows it's the last gulp of fumes it's ever going to get. The air was gray and warm and Cindy was sleeping with her mouth close to my shoulder, her little puffs of breath hitting my skin like ice on a raw nerve.

I gathered up my clothes and made it out of the room without waking her. Went into the kitchen to start the coffee, but saw it was only 0530, and damn if I didn't flash back to that patrol we'd made along the Al-Furat River, that time we stopped for MREs under the date palm and you said, "Any of you morons know that you're sitting in the cradle of humanity right now?"

I think it was Austin that said, "Damn shallow cradle for all of humanity."

That's when you told us the river's other name was the Euphrates, one of the four rivers where the Garden of Eden is supposed to have been, and you started going on about whether it happened five thousand years ago or fifty thousand or whatever, and for a while we all sat there staring at the water until Moser broke out singing that old Chicago song, "Does Anybody Really Know What Time It Is?" and every one of us started laughing and joined in on the chorus.

Anyway, that morning I'm standing there with a coffee filter in my hand and I'm staring at my coffeemaker and that song keeps beating through my brain till it's the only thing I'm thinking, and my body's getting tenser and tenser and I know I'm going to start screaming if I don't do something. The only thing I can think to do is to run. So I scratch a quick note to Cindy telling her I'm going for a jog, then I put on my running shoes and head out into the gray morning.

I must've done three or four miles before that fucking song drained out of me and I no longer felt like my head was going to explode. I actually enjoyed the run back to the house, though I had to slow to a walk a few times to catch my breath. The light was coming up pink and orange in the east, and being out there in the quiet with just the trees and the smell of grass coming off people's yards—man, it felt good.

The moment I went in through the pantry door I smelled the chocolate cupcakes, and when I peeked in the kitchen I saw a dozen of them cooling on wax paper on the table, and Cindy was shaking about a gallon of cooked macaroni in a colander over the sink. She smiled at me and said, "You haven't done that in a while. You want a glass of cold water?"

I nodded, so she hit the faucet and let it run a bit, then filled a glass half full, shoved it under the icemaker on the fridge, then handed it to me. She said, "There'll be hot dogs and burgers there, the rest is potluck. Should we take our own ketchup and mustard or will they have all that too?"

I'm standing there trying not to look too confused by all this, taking in the cupcakes and the macaroni and the big plastic bowl with the chopped celery and pickles and mayonnaise in it, and our biggest cooler open against the wall and the paper plates and plastic cups lined up on the counter.

But I guess I wasn't very successful in not looking confused, because after Cindy dumped the macaroni into the plastic bowl, she smiled again and said, "You do remember the community picnic today, right? Labor Day?"

Sometimes I look at her and feel like I've never seen her before. Like I've been dropped in from outer space or something. Like I've woken up inside somebody else's life.

She blew out a breath and said, "You don't even listen to me half the time, do you?"

"You told me about this?"

"A dozen times at least. It's all the girls have talked about all week."

"Okay," I said. "I guess it's starting to sound a little bit familiar."

She shook her head and mixed the macaroni salad. Then she scooped up some on her mixing spoon and held it up to my mouth. "Tell me if there's enough mayonnaise to suit you."

It tasted like hell first thing in the morning, but I told her it was fine. She snapped the plastic lid on and put the bowl in the refrigerator. She said, "The only other thing I thought I'd make was the Jell-O bowl you like."

"With the fruit cocktail in it?"

"I was thinking a can of pineapple chunks, plus I have a couple of bananas and an apple I want to cut up."

"Perfect," I said.

"By the time I get that done and the cupcakes iced, the girls will be up and wanting breakfast."

"What do you need me to do?"

"There's supposed to be a couple of inflatable pools for the kids. Should we let the girls take their swimsuits or not?"

"You mean like wading pools? Who all is going to be there?"

"It's in the courthouse square," she said. "Do you remember *anything* I told you?"

"So that would be like . . . hundreds of kids possibly."

"First of all, they aren't wading pools. They're fairly big, from what I hear. But every kid in town won't be in them at the same time, Russell. And the girls are going to want to get wet."

"How could I not know anything about this?" I said.

"You've had things on your mind. It's okay. I understand."

The way she said that, I wanted to sit down and cry. My chest started feeling heavy again, and the kitchen started getting tight and warm. I mean, I never knew guilt could feel like this. Guilt and shame and, I can't think of the right word for it. Is there a word for when you feel so unbelievably stupid for something you've done, and so unbelievably sorry, and so unbelievably afraid because there's nothing you can do to undo it, and right there in front of you is one of the people you love most in all the world and she doesn't know a thing about how badly you've fucked up, she still loves you and thinks you're someone special and what are you supposed to do, Spence? What's a guy supposed to do when he can't think or even fucking breathe because of one stupid fucking moment of stupidity?

She said, "I told Pops to be ready by eleven."

I nodded. Drank a little more of the water and swallowed hard. Those bits of macaroni felt like shrapnel in my stomach.

Cindy must've seen the look on my face, the way I was wincing probably, because she smiled at me and said, "Let's try to forget about everything else today, okay? Let's enjoy being a family and living in a nice town with good people around us."

It sounded like a fine suggestion, and I did my best to follow through with it, I really did. But that heaviness in my chest wouldn't go away. I went through the motions okay, I guess, did all the right stuff for the next few hours or so, even though I felt like one part of me was a robot and the other part was standing off to the side watching me and shaking his head in disgust. We might even have gotten home that day with Cindy's optimism still intact if it hadn't been for the girl. It happened around two or three that afternoon. I'm not at all sure about the time of it. All I know is that I suddenly got dizzy. I thought for sure I was going to pass out. But then I looked up and saw her. The girl and the two guys with her, all of them looking my way across the courthouse lawn.

*

"I feel the world go black and heavy."

Do you remember when you said those words to me? We were sitting in the chow hall one night, nobody but you and me, eating bowls of cherry cobbler with milk poured over it. I asked how you always managed to know an RPG was coming, the way you had that afternoon, and it wasn't the first time either. You'd yell "Incoming!" before there was any sound at all, any flash or movement to be seen. And what you told me in the chow hall was, "Right before it happens, I feel the world go black and heavy."

Of course when it happened to me at the picnic, when I saw that girl and the two guys with her checking me out, I didn't put the feeling together with anything from Iraq. I felt a terrible heaviness all of a sudden, so sad and hopeless that it made me go all weak and dizzy. And then a shiver went through me. Gee used to say that a shiver happens when somebody is walking across your grave, and that pretty much sums up the feeling, doesn't it? Like you're trapped in a box wrapped up in heavy darkness and you know that life is up there in the sunlight somewhere, a place you can never reach.

Before that, everybody had been having a really nice time at the picnic. Right away Pops found some of his buddies to throw rubber horseshoes with on the short, one-way street that'd been blocked off for the day. And the girls were jumping back and forth from the bouncy house to one of the inflatable pools to the cupcakes and back to the bouncy house. I'd been focusing on them and nothing else, Cindy and me taking turns keeping an eye on the girls, checking on Pops every now and then, bringing him a plate of food and a cold drink. I was able for a while to sort of borrow from everybody else's happiness and innocence.

Around two o'clock or so a local bluegrass group started setting up on the bandstand on the back lawn, pinging and twanging midway between where Pops was throwing horseshoes and where the girls were squealing and laughing inside the bouncy house. And then out of nowhere that awful feeling hit me, and it was exactly like you said. The air seemed to thicken and pinch in on me, and the light went dim and gray. I actually looked up and away from the bouncy house, looked to see if some big black cloud was crossing the sun. But there was nothing, the sky was as clear and washed-out blue as always. And then that icy shiver hit, and something told me to turn and look back at the bandstand.

There was Donnie grinning like an idiot, holding a canned soda in one hand and pointing across the lawn at me with the other. The girl standing beside him was already holding her sunglasses up off her eyes and squinting in my direction, and then the two guys with her turned their eyes on me too.

I put my back to them and stood there looking in through the bouncy house window at the girls. They were in there with five or six other little kids, all of them bouncing and laughing and crashing into each other like it was the greatest thing in the world. Meanwhile there's an icy shiver still crawling up and down my spine. Cindy is there beside me saying "Not so hard, girls," and "Watch your head!" and things like that. And I can feel that RPG bearing down on me from out of nowhere and without a sound.

"Excuse me, sir," the one guy says.

Every muscle in my body seizes up with dread, but I make myself turn and look at him. He's at least in his fifties, not a big guy but wiry and hard, and he has a full head of short gray hair and eyes as blue as river ice. He's smiling when I turn, and he keeps smiling all the time, that type of smile like he thinks everybody but him is a joke of some kind.

He says, "Donnie tells me you did a tour in the Mideast a few years back."

And now Cindy turns around too. I tell the guy, "Personally I wouldn't trust anything Donnie says. But in this case he's right."

"I was wondering about those desert boots GIs wear," he says. "You must have a pair of those, am I correct?"

"Had a pair," I tell him, and I can feel Cindy's eyes on me now. I can feel the question she's thinking.

That's when the other guy takes a sheet of folded-up paper from his pocket and opens it up and holds it in front of me. The paper has two images on it. The one on top was probably copied off the Internet. It shows a pair of tan desert boots, with the right boot standing upright and the left boot turned to show the Panama tread pattern. Below that image is one he probably took with his cell phone. It's a snapshot of a muddy boot print on a linoleum floor. That boot print has the same tread pattern as in the top image.

This other guy is bigger and younger than the wiry one, going soft in the middle, kind of sloppy looking. As for the girl with them, I feel her gaze on me but I can't bring myself to meet it.

The sloppy guy says, "Some GIs who are bikers like to wear their boots when they ride."

I say, "Is that more of Donnie's questionable wisdom?"

The wiry guy says, "I hear they're really comfortable. You know of a place I can get a pair?"

I say, "How about the place where you got that picture of them?"

The wiry guy takes the sheet of paper from the other one, looks at it and smiles, then hands it to Cindy. She's too confused to do anything but take it from him and look at it.

The wiry guy smiles at me and says, "Well, if you think of anything, let Shelley know, okay? She says the two of you are old friends."

I'd like to look at the girl now but I'm afraid to take my eyes off the wiry guy. He gives Cindy another big smile. "These bouncy houses are great exercise for kids, aren't they? Your girls will sleep like babies when they get home."

And then all three of them turn and walk away. I'm angry and scared at the same time. I'm breathing like I can't get any air into my lungs, and I know Cindy is looking at me, waiting, but it's only when I start hearing the kids squealing and laughing again that I realize I've been standing in a kind of soundless vacuum for I don't know how long, a place where the only sounds that registered on me were what those two guys had to say. I feel exactly like I did after the propane tank exploded. I couldn't have been more stunned.

"Russell," Cindy finally says.

I turn to her, and she holds up the sheet of paper and says, "What's going on here?"

"I'll be back in a minute," I say, and I take the piece of paper from her hand, I'm not sure why, and I go marching over to where Donnie and Cindy's mother are standing in front of the bandstand. I'm moving so fast that I bump into Donnie's can of soda and some of it splashes up onto my shirt and I smell the whiskey in it.

"Who are those guys?" I ask him, too loud for where we were.

"Who—the McClaine boys?"

"They're brothers?" I ask.

"Always used to be," he says, and he grins like he thinks he's funny.

"What did you tell them about me?"

"They asked a couple of questions is all, and I answered them."

Janice says, "Donnie wouldn't ever tell anything on you you didn't want told."

He grins and says, "Not for free anyway."

"You don't know anything about me, you understand? You keep your fucking mouth shut."

"Whoa, hey, there's kids around."

I move even closer then, right up against him. "Cindy doesn't want you here, you understand what I'm saying? Am I getting through to you? She doesn't want you anywhere near her or the girls. And what she doesn't want, I don't want."

He says, "Now Russell. A man's got the right to see his own grandchildren."

"A man does," I tell him. "But you don't."

And I'm shaking all the way back to Cindy. Because the worst, I know, is about to come.

I've got my eyes on her and she's got hers on me, and I'm walking slow and as steady as I can and trying to figure out what the hell I'm going to tell her. It's time for a reckoning, I know that. I know I owe it to her and I know she's going to demand it now.

But what I can't figure out, Spence, couldn't then and still can't now, is where's the line between total honesty and lying for a good reason? She's the first person I ever met who I thought I could be totally honest with, and wanted to be, and promised to be, and was until that day I had a muddy naked woman in my arms.

I kept a lot of stuff from Mom and Gee and Pops over the years. And from you too. Stuff that mainly made me ashamed of myself. Looking back on it now, I can see how trivial most of it was, like stealing change out of Pops' jar. But I like to think I could have told all of you everything and you wouldn't have judged me harshly for it. If I didn't believe that, I wouldn't be unloading on you now. I only wish I could hear you say something back to me. I wish these one-sided conversations we're having could bring me a little clarity and forgiveness.

I don't know that I ever really told you about the day Mom had her accident. I wasn't yet nine years old. Second grade. I'd get off the bus some three hundred yards or so from where we were living then. Anyway . . . I don't know why I got started on this. The word "reckoning," I guess. The first time I remember hearing that word was the Sunday after I came home from school and found Mom lying at the bottom of the basement stairs. She'd managed to scoop up some of the wet clothes from the basket she'd been hauling up the stairs before she slipped, and she was laying there with some wet towels and stuff bunched up under her head, barely conscious, with one knee shattered, one wrist broken, and that damage to her back that three spinal fusions only seemed to make worse. Anyway, that Sunday, Gee insisted I go to church with her so we could pray together that Mom would be all right. "Like new," she told me. "We're going to pray that God and the doctors will make her like new again."

Unfortunately, Rev. Miller's sermon that day was about "the reckoning that none can escape." On the way home I asked Gee what kind of wrecking it was going to be. Could it happen in a school bus, for example? Would it happen when I was on my bike?

She explained that the word was three syllables, not two, and that it meant a final judgment. The day when every soul is called to account for its sins.

And that's what I was remembering at the community picnic when I was walking back toward Cindy in a kind of slow-motion haze. This is my reckoning, I kept thinking. But it's not even the final one. This was only the Cindy reckoning. There was also bound to be a McClaine reckoning. And probably a Donnie reckoning of some kind, though in truth I was actually looking forward to that one. Most likely there'd be a Pops reckoning too. And maybe even a legal reckoning, which actually

made me sick to my stomach that day because of the courthouse loom-
ing above me.

It's funny how many fears and thoughts and agonies can go crashing through your brain while you're walking in a slow-motion haze
toward the woman you love.

"Oh honey," Gee had told me back when I was little and scared
and thinking me and everybody I loved was going to have some kind
of wreck like my mother did. She reached out while she was driving
to squeeze my hand. "Not wrecking. Rec-kon-ing. They mean entirely
different things."

But what she failed to mention was that they feel pretty much the
same.

*

"You need to tell me what's going on," Cindy said.

I looked into the bouncy house to see how the girls were doing.
Emma was sitting in one corner, bouncing up and down on her butt
while Dani and the other kids kept trampolining from wall to wall.

To Cindy I said, "Now's not the place or time for that."

She reached down then and took hold of my right hand and lifted
it toward her. It was only then I realized I was still holding the sheet of
paper, but all balled up in my fist now. She pulled back my fingers and
pried the paper loose and opened it up again, looked at it for a second
and then grabbed me around the wrist and dragged me back behind the
bouncy house. There was an empty space of maybe four feet between
the bouncy house and the courthouse, with a long orange extension
cord running from the bouncy house power unit to an electrical outlet
carved into a granite block. The hum from the blower that kept the
bouncy house inflated made a low, steady echo against the granite.

Cindy said, "Who were those men? And what's this about you and
that Shelley being friends?"

"I never saw those guys before today."

She held the paper up in front of my face. "You have these boots," she said. "Are these your footprints?"

"They could be," I answered "Or they could be a million other guys'."

"Where was this picture taken?"

"Cindy, come on. We'll talk about this at home."

"How do you know her? Were you in her house?"

"It's not what you think."

"My father knows, doesn't he? Do you want me to ask him?"

I moved closer and put my hands on her shoulders. She's as rigid and cold as a slab of stone. "Sweetheart. Listen. I swear to God. I met that girl once for maybe five minutes. I said maybe ten words to her total. Nothing happened. And nothing ever would. I swear that to you on my children's souls."

She was blowing one quick breath after another out between her lips. And then her eyes started to tear up and her body sagged a little beneath my hands. "You and the girls are my life," I told her. "The only life I will ever want or ever need."

Bit by bit her breaths got slower, every exhalation a little longer than the last. Finally she broke eye contact with me, looked at the back of the bouncy house for a few seconds. Then she folded up the piece of paper and slipped it into her hip pocket. She said, "I think it's time we pack things up and head back home."

"I couldn't agree more," I said.

*

We drove home from the picnic without much talking, same as I expected we would. Every now and then Cindy would turn around and ask the girls a question, like what was the favorite thing you did today? Something that would get them chattering again for a few minutes.

Pops sat in the back with a girl on each side of him, hugging up against him. Sometimes he would tickle one of them and I'd get startled by a quick burst of giggles.

Most of the way to Pops' place I followed an Escalade moving maybe forty miles per hour tops, so it didn't take me long to start hating the driver and the vehicle itself. What the hell is an escalade anyway? I wondered. I know what an escapade is, and I know what it means to escalate, but the word "escalade" did not make any sense to me. In fact I got so impatient with the driver in front of me, who seemed to think it was necessary to slow down and tap his brakes every twenty feet or so, that I finally started thinking out loud. Pops surprised me by knowing the answer to my question.

He said, "You've probably seen a dozen movies with escalades in them."

"Like this stupid Cadillac in front of me? That's the only kind I've ever seen."

"You never seen soldiers trying to climb into a castle or a fort using ladders?"

"Yeah. And most times they get burning oil dumped on them."

"That's called an escalade. Trying to scale a wall with ladders. It's where the word 'escalator' comes from."

Cindy turned halfway in her seat and gave Pops a big smile. "I'm impressed," she said.

He said, "I tend to have that effect on the ladies. Right, girls?"

"I still don't see what that has to do with a vehicle," I said. "What wall is that vehicle climbing?"

"What does Lumina have to do with my little car?" he asked. "What that word really means is the open space inside my intestines."

"Ewww!" Dani said, which was probably the effect Pops was going for.

"How do you know all these words?" Cindy asked.

"You didn't know I'm such a brainy guy, did you, sweetie? Truth is, I've been playing a lot of Scrabble with a former English professor. She whups me good every time, but at least I'm learning a thing or two from my beatings. It's got so that now, every time I hear a word I don't know, I look it up."

Cindy said, "Maybe that's something you should try, Russell."

"What? Playing Scrabble?"

She said, "No. Learning a little something."

For Cindy to say that in front of the girls and Pops, it hit me like a slap. My face went red and hot. And I realized then how angry at me she still was. She was still stinging from being humiliated at the picnic, from the suggestion that I'd been cheating on her. She'd been stewing about that the same as I'd been stewing about those McClaine brothers and what their next move might be.

So I sat there with my mouth clamped shut and my stomach churning until I pulled up in front of Pops' place. Then I told her, "I'll be right back. I need to make a pit stop."

In the lobby I gave Pops a quick hug and told him, "I'm going to hit the head. I'll call you in a day or so."

Then I hustled down the hall to the men's room and made it into a stall maybe half a second before I started throwing up. I gagged and spit until I felt like crying.

When I came back out of the stall to wash up, there was Pops leaning against the wall. "I'm fine," I told him. "Something I ate, I guess."

"I ate the same things you did, Rusty."

Him calling me Rusty again, which he hadn't done since before I went into the Army, made my stomach buckle. I turned on the tap and rinsed out my mouth.

He tore a couple sheets of paper towel off the dispenser and walked over and handed them to me. "Don't make the mistake of thinking I don't know you," he said. "I know you like the back of my hand."

I took the paper towels and wiped my face off. I still couldn't look him in the eye, so I looked at myself in the mirror. "What do you know about a couple of brothers named McClaine?" I said.

"I saw those boys at the picnic today," Pops said.

"That's why I'm asking."

"What do they have to do with you?"

"I'm trying to find that out. Can you tell me what you know about them?"

"I know I wouldn't want you messin' with them."

"I'm not but I think Donnie is. He pointed me out to them today. Then they wanted to know if I have a pair of desert boots. They had a picture of tread marks off somebody's floor. Trying to track somebody down, I guess."

"That piece of shit Donnie would turn on his own mother if there was a dollar in it for him."

"You're not telling me anything I don't already know."

Pops leaned up against a sink and gave me a hard look. "You have a pair of those boots."

"Me and a few thousand other guys, yeah. But you still haven't told me anything about those brothers."

"They're like Donnie except meaner and nastier. Neither one of them's ever worked an honest day in his life."

"What are they into?"

"Whatever they can get their fingers in. Started out, I seem to remember, rolling Amish guys. They was arrested for that. Both did a little time, but not enough. I don't like judging a man on rumor but those two are an exception. And over the years, rumor's had them involved with everything from pimping to assault to breaking and entering to dealing. These days they always manage to skate, though. Learned a thing or two in prison, I guess. Or one of them did. That would be Phil, the older one. The other one's Howard, goes by Bubby. He's more than a little light on the intellect."

111

I nodded. Couldn't think of anything else to do or say.

"What do they got against you?"

"I wish I knew."

He kept looking at me. Not that I could see him doing it, but I could sure enough feel it, even as I stood there staring down at the faucet. It was made of brass and getting that bluish crust along the joints and seams. The longer I stared at it the harder it was to look away.

Finally he straightened up. "Whatever it is, don't let it get out of hand."

"There's nothing to get out of hand, Pops."

He nodded once. Then turned and headed for the door. "Nip it in the bud, son. If I taught you anything, I taught you that."

When he walked out, it felt like he took all the air out with him. He had me for a liar, I'd seen it in his eyes right from the start. One bad decision, and now this. I wanted to put my fist through that face in the mirror.

*

Cindy never said a word about the incident at the picnic until she came to bed that night. I was already in bed, stiff as a board underneath the cotton sheet. She came out of the bathroom wearing a full set of summer pajamas, which I knew right there was a bad sign. Plus she left the bathroom light on, then also turned on the table lamp on the nightstand. And tossed that sheet of paper down on my chest.

"You plan to tell me or what?" she said. "Cause if you're not, you might as well get out of my bed right now."

I took the paper and crumpled it up and dropped it off the side of the bed. Then I rolled toward her and pulled the covers back. "Turn the lights out and come lay down," I said.

It took her a few seconds to move, but she finally did. She flicked off the bathroom light, then the table lamp. Then she climbed in, rolled onto her side and looked me square in the eyes. "Why'd you lie about having those boots?"

A long, slow breath came out of my mouth then. It felt like surrender, which I knew I had to do.

"Remember that day I got caught in the rain coming home from work?"

"What about it?"

"That was the day I found out the plant was closing. I had to take a new way home because of an accident on the main road. It was mostly farmland, second-growth timber, a few houses here and there . . ."

"And?"

"I'm taking it fairly easy in the rain because the roads are slick. And I pass this one house, out in the middle of nowhere. A little cottage is all it is. Some kind of mongrel dog chained up to the front porch. But there's music blasting out of the house, I can hear it from the road. And there's this woman in the yard. Turning circles in the mud and the rain. Dancing, I guess."

"What kind of a woman?"

"That one at the picnic today. With the two guys."

"So you stopped?"

"No! I mean I did, but only because she slipped in the mud and fell down flat on her back. So I slowed down and kept watching and she never got up. Never even moved. So yeah, I stopped. If she was hurt, you know, I couldn't ride away and leave her lying there."

"Was she hurt?"

"I really don't know. She was high as a kite on something. I mean . . . she was outside dancing, and she was . . ."

"She was what, Russell?"

"She didn't have any clothes on."

"What!" she said.

I just nodded.

"What did you do?"

"I asked if she was okay, but I couldn't understand much of what she said."

"Did you call 911?"

"I should have. That's what I should've done. But she was trying to get up then and said something about me carrying her inside."

"I thought you couldn't understand her."

"Most of it I couldn't. A word here and there is all. But she kept reaching up to me and saying what I thought was, 'Take me inside. Take me inside.' So I picked her up and carried her inside."

"She was completely naked and you picked her up?"

"Sweetie, what was I supposed to do? Let her lay there hurt?"

"How did you pick her up?"

"One hand under her shoulders, one hand under her knees."

"And then what?"

"Then I carried her inside."

"Where inside?"

"The front room was like . . . nothing but a couple of chairs and a TV set. So I took a look in the nearest room and there was a mattress on the floor, so I laid her down on it."

"Nothing but a mattress?"

"A single old mattress, that's it. I kept asking if she was okay, if she wanted me to call anybody, but all she did was to keep smiling, you know? It didn't seem like she was in any pain."

"So you what? You left her there?"

"I honestly didn't know what else to do. She seemed fine physically, other than being sky-high on something. And that house, I don't know, it felt strange to me. It wasn't a place people lived. So I'm thinking about you, I'm thinking about the girls. I'm thinking whatever this place is, I don't want to be seen here. So yeah, I left. I got my ass out of there and back home to you."

"And that's it?" she said.

"That's it. I swear."

"It was your boot prints on the floor?"

"Probably."

"So what do they care for? Those men. If that's all that happened. They should be grateful to you. Not looking like they want to hurt somebody."

"All I can figure is they came home and found her there, probably sleeping it off on the mattress, mud everywhere, some man's boot prints leading into the room where she is, and they jumped to the wrong conclusions. I don't know if you noticed or not, but she had a pretty good-size bruise on her face. Somebody had laid into her for some reason."

Cindy was silent awhile, looking at me but not looking at me, if you know what I mean. Convincing herself to believe me, you know? And I want her to believe me, Spence. More than anything in the world I want that. Even though I'm sick to my stomach for not telling her the whole truth.

So finally she says, "So now what?"

"Now nothing," I say.

"Are you sure? What about those men?"

"They were fishing, that's all. I'm guessing that girl mentioned that the guy who helped her was on a motorcycle. And they matched up the boot prints with GI desert boots. But that's all they know. That's all they'll ever know."

"So how'd they match the boots and the motorcycle with you?"

"Your fucking father, that's how. I'm sorry, I didn't mean to swear. But I saw him pointing me out to them. Apparently he knows them. I can even hear that slimy you-know-what. 'Hey, my son-in-law has boots like that. Hey, my son-in-law rides a motorcycle.'"

"I saw you talking to him."

"I know you did. I'm not trying to hide anything here."

A few moments passed. Then she laid a hand against my chest. "Every time I see him I get sick to my stomach."

"That makes two of us. I told him you don't want him around. I told him I better never see him anywhere near this place again."

I thought she might have a few more questions for me, but she didn't. The thing about Cindy is, she knows what she has, and she knows she wants to keep it. She slid up closer and laid her head against my shoulder. I put my arm around her and buried my nose and mouth in her hair. Her scent went into me like light into darkness.

The only problem was, I knew the darkness was still there. I knew it was all around us now. And I knew who had invited it in.

*

First grade started for Dani the day after Labor Day. On Friday of that week I had a job interview with Lowe's in the afternoon—nothing special, wear a red vest and a name tag and help people find the lightbulb aisle, that kind of thing—so Cindy had to get off work early to pick up Dani. There's an afterschool program at the school she goes to, though; they hire a couple of high schoolers to watch the little ones until four in the afternoon, keeping them active on the playground or on rainy days in the gym. But on Friday those extra minutes or so of playtime brought Cindy as close to a breakdown, and me too in a different kind of way, as either of us ever wants to come.

Cindy pulled into the parking lot a few minutes before four, she said, and she recognized Phil McClaine through the chain-link fence the moment she saw him. He was pushing Dani and a few other kids on the merry-go-round. Pushing nice and easy, Cindy told me later, not super fast or dangerous, but that didn't keep her from flying into a panic and running onto the playground past the high-school girl who was standing there texting somebody. Cindy grabbed up Dani, and once she had her safe and sound, she turned on McClaine and said, "What are you doing here?"

Cindy said he kept right on smiling and pushing the merry-go-round and said, "She sure is a pretty girl, Cindy. Takes after her mother."

The man is evil, Spence. My blood runs cold just writing this now. Imagine what Cindy was feeling at the time. I know you never had kids but I also know you wanted them. I remember you talking about it on several occasions.

Anyway, Cindy told him, "You stay away from my children! If I ever see you here again—"

He turned away from the merry-go-round then, which made Cindy jump back a little. And he said, "I imagine you have to run over to Baker Street to pick up Emma now, right? So I'll tell you ladies goodbye. I hope you had fun, Dani. I did. And don't forget; tell your daddy I need to have a little talk with him, okay?"

Then he walked away grinning, Cindy said. Sauntered over to the parking lot and up to his truck. Got in and drove away.

You can bet that Cindy gave the high-school girl an earful. She even went inside to the office and demanded they enforce some kind of security system so that nobody gets into that playground but parents and kids. But she didn't want to waste a lot of time in there, she wanted to get over to the daycare and make sure Emma was okay.

It was maybe thirty minutes later I pulled into the driveway on my bike, and within fifteen seconds there was Cindy in the garage with me, standing up close and practically screaming at me in a hoarse whisper about what had happened. I didn't even have time to get off the bike.

And I lost it. How did that asshole know where to find my babies? He must have been watching us, following us, figuring out when to pull that kind of shit. I swear, Spence, the whole time we were together over in Iraq, I never felt such red-hot hatred or anger for anybody. But there in my garage, even though there was still plenty of daylight streaming in, everything went tight and black on me except for Cindy's face, and it was so strained with fear that I barely recognized her.

I popped the bike into neutral and shoved it backward out of the garage so fast I nearly laid it down twice, but then got turned and thumbed down the starter and was out on the street again. Cindy was back there in the garage holding her belly and screaming at me to come back, but I couldn't stop myself. I was pure hatred and nothing else. Nothing but blind, stupid hatred with murder in my eyes.

The only place I knew to look for him was the meth house. If I got there and the place was empty, I was going to tear it apart board by board looking for his address. At one point it occurred to me that Pops might know where McClaine lived—I mean hell, he was probably in the phone book, or I could track him down online—but I didn't want to stop or turn around and take the time for anything more sensible. I wanted to kill that motherfucker.

Lucky for him, or maybe for me, I didn't know the back road well enough to be flying along at sixty miles an hour. I missed a turn, bounced up over a drainage ditch and went flying into the bushes. I don't remember if it was the ground or a tree or what that put me out, I only remember coming to with the sun in my eyes, a bee buzzing over me, and a whole lot of pain in my left shoulder and arm, ribs, and the side of my head.

It was the phone ringing and vibrating in my pocket that brought me back to my senses. Cindy, of course. All I told her was that I'd taken a spill and didn't think the bike was going to start, and maybe she should load the ramp onto the truck and come and get me. She had the good sense to call Pops while she was gathering up the girls. He was a full ten minutes closer to me than she was, and by the time Cindy and the girls arrived, I was already sitting in his car, hurting like hell with every breath, and still too shaky to wipe the blood off my face and arms.

Cindy started crying when she saw me, and though I wanted more than anything to go home, she told Pops in no uncertain terms that she was taking me straight to the hospital. He got the truck backed up over the drainage ditch, then he and Cindy muscled the bike up the ramp while the girls watched from inside the truck, and I watched all of them through the side mirror of Pops' Lumina.

Talk about feeling stupid. I still planned to go after McClaine first chance I got, but in my current condition I stood about as much chance against him as a hamster.

Once the bike was loaded up, Pops came to the car to tell me he and Cindy were swapping vehicles and that she would drive me to the hospital, but I begged him to take me himself. So he made up a story about the brakes on his Lumina going bad, and in the end he and I led the way in the Lumina, with Cindy, the girls, and my banged-up bike bringing up the rear.

*

On the way to the hospital, me all balled up in pain leaning against the passenger side, Pops didn't waste any time getting down to brass tacks. "What the hell is going on here, son? She said you went flying off like a madman."

"Did she tell you why?"

"More or less."

"I couldn't sit by and do nothing, could I?"

"So instead you fly off half-cocked and nearly break your neck."

Pops always did have a way of going straight to the heart of things. I felt like a little kid again with him scolding me like that.

He said, "You need to tell me what's going on between you and those McClaine boys. And you need to tell me right now."

So I did. I told him the whole story. Even what I'd left out in the version I told Cindy.

He never said a word for the next few miles. In fact, he didn't so much as look at me again until we pulled up at the emergency entrance. Then he shut off the engine, got out and fast-walked into the hospital. A minute later, while I was still trying to climb out of the car, he comes out pushing a wheelchair, walking so fast the nurse has a hard time keeping up with him.

I got to admit I was kind of relieved to be wheeled off to X-ray before Cindy and the girls showed up.

About an hour later I'm in a hospital bed with my ribs taped and about a quart of iodine or some other orange stuff swabbed all over my cheek and arm. I must've looked like some kind of Apache daubed up with war paint. Then they let Cindy and the girls in to see me, while Pops went off looking for coffee that didn't come out of a vending machine.

There wasn't much Cindy could say about how stupid I was, not with the girls there wanting to crawl up beside me and kiss all my boo-boos. The look in her eyes said more than enough, though. She knew I had failed them, and so did I. But she didn't know how big a failure I really was.

They stayed maybe an hour or so with me. But the girls hadn't had any supper yet, so even though Cindy wanted to stay, she kissed me goodnight and said they'd be back in the morning.

I told her, "They might turn me loose tomorrow, babe. Why don't you wait until I talk to the doc or whoever. I'll give you a call when I know something."

I almost broke down with the three of them hugging and kissing me and saying how much they loved me. God, Spence, I felt like such an idiot. You would have chewed me out good if you'd been there. Probably would've ripped me a new asshole, as we used to say.

Anyway, the girls weren't gone more than a minute before Pops came back in. And he got right down to it.

"What now?" he said.

"I need to take the money back to them."

He rubbed his cheek again, the way he sometimes does when he's thinking. Then he said, "A few years back there was this young fella named Decarlo, Decario, something like that. Played football out at

Ohio State. Supposed to be pretty good at it too. So he's home one summer, and apparently he got to fooling around with that girl. The one you scooped up out of the mud. Next thing the kid knows, he's arrested for raping her. Now I'm not saying he did it or didn't. There's only two people know that for sure. What I do know is that right before the case goes to trial, the charges get dropped. A week later the boy's family's house goes up for sale. From what I hear, they took quite a beating on it."

"You think it was a scam? She suckered the kid in?"

"I'm saying I don't think giving back the money is going to solve your problems. If I'm thinking like a McClaine, I'm thinking you're only giving back what was mine to begin with. I'm thinking I'm going to want something more. Something of yours."

They had me hooked up to one of those heart monitors, Spence, so it wasn't long before a nurse came in to see why my heart was racing like I'd sprinted ten miles uphill with a full pack.

"You having a hard time breathing?" she asked.

"This tape might be a little tight."

"It's supposed to be tight. I'll get you something for the pain."

As soon as she was out the door, I looked at Pops and said, "So what are my options here?"

He said, "I'm trying to think of one."

Then the nurse was back with a plastic bag of something, which she rigged up to drip into the tube already taped to my arm. "You'll start feeling better in a minute or so," she said. "You might want to tell your grandfather goodnight while you're still awake."

She hung around so long after that, watching the monitor and taking my pulse, that before I knew it I was having a hard time keeping my eyes open. I'd feel myself going off into the dark, sort of slowly melting down into it, then I'd yank myself back up again and force my eyes open. But then the dark would take hold of me again and suck me back down.

The last thing I remember is feeling Pops' stubbly chin scrape against my nose as he kissed me on the forehead. I tried to lift my arms up and hug him, but I was in the quicksand then, brother, and sort of hoping I'd never have to come back out.

The doctor didn't get around to having a look at me until after eleven the next morning. Cindy had already called three times for an update. Good thing it was a Saturday; she didn't have to go to work or take the girls anywhere.

After the doc released me I sent Cindy a text, cause I wasn't ready yet to get into a conversation with her. I knew that was waiting for me at home once the girls were busy playing or watching TV. I got dressed and went downstairs and signed some papers, then I went outside and sat on a bench overlooking the parking lot. All I could think about was how much that night in the hospital was going to cost me. Three, four thousand minimum, that was my guess. Shit, they charge you fifty dollars every time they step inside the room.

So Cindy pulls up in the truck, and the girls aren't with her, so I know I'm in for it. No way she'd leave the girls with anybody on a weekend unless she has serious business to attend to. I climb in and shut the door and sit there watching the telephone poles go by.

We're nearly halfway home before she swings us off the road and into a Food Lion parking lot. She eases into the first empty slot and shuts off the engine. She sniffs a couple of times, and it finally dawns on me she's crying. It hurts to look at her sitting there hunched up over the steering wheel.

"I didn't do anything with that girl," I tell her.

"You did something," she says.

And there it was again, another chance to come clean and tell her about the money. Looking back, I can see these moments clear as day. But when you're actually inside one of them, and there's this heavy fog over everything you do and say and think, it's not so easy to make an intelligent decision. I'd already disappointed her once. How would she react to finding out her husband was a thief? I felt hollow and broken and more alone than I'd ever felt in my life. The rest of the truth could only make matters worse.

So I told her, "I swear to God I didn't."

"That man threatened one of our babies!"

"I've been thinking about that. And I think all he wanted was to scare you. You and me both."

"Well he did a pretty damn good job of it, didn't he?"

"He's not going to touch them, I know he won't. How stupid would that be if he did? The playground monitor saw him, the vice principal knows he was there. You put it all on record."

"So maybe he's too stupid to think about that. Then what?"

"He's not stupid, Cindy. He's calculating. Pops told me about how the three of them shook down a college kid by charging him with rape."

"Oh my God, Russell."

"It won't happen with us, I promise you. There's no evidence. Not a shred. Things are different these days, what with DNA and forensics and all that stuff. Plus, if they try the same scam again, their history will come back to haunt them. We'll take *them* to court."

"With what? How are we supposed to pay a lawyer? I don't even know how we're going to pay your hospital bill!"

"I took care of that already." I don't know why I said it, Spence. Because I love her, I guess. And because I'd already caused her enough worry.

"What do you mean you took care of it? *How?*"

"Your insurance covered about a third of it. The rest was covered by some program for low-income families. With me being out of work and all."

At first she seemed pleased by this news. Then she broke down and started crying for real. "Damn it, Russell. What's next for us—food stamps? I will not live like that again!"

"You won't have to, babe. I promise. If I don't get that job at Lowe's, I'll find something else. I'll flip burgers if I have to. You and the girls are my life. You know that."

Finally she pinched the tears from her eyes and rubbed her cheeks dry. "I forgot to ask you how the interview went yesterday."

"Good," I told her. "Real good. He said I'd hear from him sometime next week."

The thing is, I'd already heard from the guy who interviewed me. He took a long look at my résumé and said, "You know, Russell, I like to hire our vets whenever I can. Male and female. The thing about you is, with this college degree, you're always going to be looking for something better. And you should have something better. So if I do what I want and hire you now, a month or so down the road, I'm going to have to fill the same position again."

Which leaves me where, Spence? Getting screwed by the elephant, that's where.

*

That first day back from the hospital, Cindy wanted me to spend the entire day on the couch, nursing my wounds like some kind of invalid. But I couldn't sit still, no matter how much my body was hurting, not even with a couple of sweet little girls crawling into my lap every ten minutes. The more love they poured over me, the more I ached to set things right. But every possible correction I could think of felt less like a correction and more like trying to cancel out a negative with another negative.

That's supposed to work in math, but I never could understand the logic behind it. Mostly all I had to know at the crushing plant was simple arithmetic. A hundred and twenty tons of this material and four hundred tons of that. Add them together and that's how much inventory we had in the yard. Subtract it from the number of tons on the purchase order, and we either had enough inventory or needed to order more. But there was no way sixty negative tons times a hundred negative tons was ever going to produce six thousand tons of anything. It doesn't work that way in real life. It can't. All you're going to end up with is a lot more of a bad thing.

All I knew for certain was that sitting around watching cartoons with my girls made me feel like a horde of ants was crawling through my veins. So when Cindy wasn't looking, I slipped out into the garage.

My bike, which was still in the bed of the pickup, was banged up pretty good. The crankcase was dripping oil onto the truck bed, the handlebars were twisted out of alignment, and the front fender was bent up against the tire. The whole left side was caked with dirt and covered with scratches.

I put up the garage door and was pulling out the ramp when I felt Cindy standing there watching me. "And what do you think you're doing?" she said.

"Trying not to go crazy from sitting still all the time."

"Well you're not ever going to ride that thing again."

"You going to drive me to Lowe's every day? Pick me up every night?"

It was the closest thing we'd ever had to a fight, Spence. I hated myself for the way I sounded.

Finally she said, "Well you can't unload it by yourself."

"I've done it dozens of times before."

"Not with bruised ribs you haven't. Where do you want me, top or bottom?"

How do you deal with a woman like that, brother? How do you do anything but love a woman like that? I honestly had tears in my eyes just looking at her.

"Stand down there and steady it for me." I said. "The tricky part is when I have to jump down without letting go of it."

I felt like my ribs were being pulled out of my side, but we finally eased the bike down and got it parked in the driveway. It hurt like hell holding in all my moans and groans the whole time.

"Thanks, babe," I told her.

She came up to me then and threw her arms around me and pressed herself up against me. "You're a damn fool," she said. "I hope you realize that."

"Time and time again," I told her.

It took some doing, but an hour or so later I had the crankcase sealed up tight again, the handlebars straightened, and the fender pulled away from the tire. Cindy and the girls came out into the garage when I fired up the engine so I could listen to the idle.

Cindy had to raise her voice to be heard over the growling pipes. "You're not planning to ride that today, I hope."

"You know what they say about falling off a horse."

"And you're a horse's ass," she said.

Dani gasped and said, "Mommy, you swore!" and Emma held to Cindy's leg and giggled.

I told her, "That's already been established."

Then I swung a leg over the seat and eased myself down. "I need a little shakedown cruise, babe. That's all. I need to take it through the gears a couple of times. Make sure I didn't knock something out of place."

She reached out then and put both hands on Dani's shoulders. "You see this?" she asked me.

I said, "I do."

Then she did the same with Emma. "You see this?"

"I do."

And she put a hand on her own belly. "You see this?"

"Of course I do."

"Then put your helmet on and make sure you're back here in time for supper."

And I was too. In fact I was a few minutes early. I didn't waste any time out at Pops' storage unit. I came back with five thousand dollars in cash, which I would use on Monday to pay off my hospital bill. I also came back with a couple of boxes of .22 longs for Pops' old revolver. My plans for them weren't yet specific.

*

Come Monday morning, Cindy headed off with Dani. She left ten minutes early so she could have "a few choice words" with the vice principal, she said. Cindy is usually a very low-key girl, always the quiet one in a crowd, but I didn't envy anybody who got in between her and her little ones. That vice principal, and anybody else within spitting range, was in for a good tongue-lashing.

My plan for the morning was to spend some time with Emma, doing whatever my little Princess wanted to do, even if it meant sipping imaginary tea with her and Pooh Bear. Then I'd call Pops and ask him to come sit with her for an hour or so while I paid a visit to the hospital. So I set Emma up at the breakfast table with some French toast with sliced bananas and a cup of milk, and went off to grab a shower and shave.

Emma and Dani both know they aren't supposed to answer the phone if it rings, or go to the door if somebody knocks. They *know* this. Which is why my heart jumped up into my throat when I stepped out of the shower and heard voices in the kitchen. I barely got the towel around my waist before busting into the kitchen like a crazy man.

I got to admit, seeing Cindy's mother, Janice, sitting there at the table with Emma was a hell of a relief, even if Donnie was over at the counter, helping himself to a cup of coffee. Janice looked up at me and grinned. "Well aren't you looking good this morning," she said.

My first thought was that Emma was safe. My second thought was that I'd already told Donnie in no uncertain terms that he wasn't welcome in my house. So I said to him, hoping to keep my voice calm enough not to scare Emma, "What are you doing here?"

He set the cup down and held up both hands. "I only dropped by for a second. There's something I need to talk about with you."

I pointed at the back door. "Outside."

Janice said, "You going outside dressed like that?"

I was too angry to answer. I went into the pantry and out the back door and waited for Donnie to follow me.

The moment the door closed behind him I said, "What did I tell you?"

"I know what you said but this is for your own benefit. I'm worried about my daughter and those little girls."

"What are you talking about?"

"I don't know what those McClaine boys have against you," he said, and before he could say another word I felt myself stepping up close to him, so close he fell back against the outside wall.

"Hold on!" he said. "I'm just delivering a message is all!"

"Then deliver it."

"All I was told is, 'He knows what he owes us.' That's all Phil said. And that he wants it back now."

"What do I owe him?" I said. I'm standing there up against him, all but naked, barefoot in the grass. He's maybe two inches taller than me in those cowboy boots he always wears, but I'm feeling so goddamn huge right then, so fiery hot and huge with rage even though every inch of my skin is bristling with goose bumps. It was unlike anything I ever felt over there with you, even in our worst moments. Over there I was almost always scared, straining to hear every noise and flicker of movement. But there in my backyard I felt, I don't know . . . so hungry for violence I was shaking. Does that make any sense to you? Did you ever feel like that?

I'm ashamed to admit there was something, and I don't use this word lightly, but something glorious about the anger and hatred I felt.

God, I wanted to tear him to pieces. I wanted to rip him apart piece by piece until I was dripping with his blood.

"I told you," he said, barely breathing now, and God how I loved how scared he looked at that moment. "I don't know nothing about nothing. All I know is what he told me. You have something of his, he says, and he wants it back."

"Or what?" I said.

"Huh?"

"What if I don't know what the fuck you're talking about? Which means I can't give him back whatever he thinks I owe him. What then?"

"Hell, Rusty," he said, and that did it for me, that finally tripped the trigger, him calling me Rusty the way Pops sometimes did. My hand shot up and around his throat so fast and hard that his head banged back against the wall. Both his hands went to my wrist, trying to pull me off, but I knew I could kill him if I wanted to. And I wanted to, Spence. I wanted to pinch his head right off him.

"You ever call me that again," I told him, "and it will be the last word you ever say."

I stood there like that another five seconds or so, feeling how easy it would have been to crush his throat and be done with him. Then I let go and stepped back. "You have five seconds to get off my property," I told him. "You don't, I'm going to finish the job right now."

He didn't say a word. Just ducked away from me and hustled toward the street, coughing all the way.

I went inside and said to Janice, "Donnie's waiting for you out on the sidewalk."

Maybe it was the way I said it, I don't know. Maybe I looked as monstrous and invincible to her as I felt. Anyway, she got up and kissed Emma goodbye and was out the door and gone.

I have never in my life felt an emotion like that one. Like I was the elephant, you know? All loaded and cocked to rape the living shit out of anybody who even dared look at me the wrong way.

And now I'm wishing you were here to tell me it was a good thing I felt that day. In fact I almost wish I was back over there with you right now, back there breathing sand every minute, working our way door to door, death waiting behind every wall and around every corner. I'd do every minute of that hell over again if I could, because if I could do that, I could come back home again in one piece, and that would change everything. I mean if there was only one single moment I could change, I got to be honest with you. As much as I wish I could see that big-toothed grin of yours again, and talk to you again in person the way we used to, I'm sorry to say I'd have to let you be. Because the moment I'd change is that wet-looking morning last summer when Cindy catches me staring out the kitchen window at a dawn sky filled with dark clouds, and she says to me, "You want me to get the girls up?" That's the moment I'd have to redo, Spence. I'd give her the biggest smile in the world and say, "Yeah, babe. You mind?"

*

The day after I nearly ripped Donnie's head off, about ten or so in the morning, somebody knocked on the back door. I was with Emma in the living room, playing under a blanket I'd stretched over the couch and coffee table. She had all of her stuffed animals in there with us, pretending like we were the Wild Thornberrys. Emma was Eliza, of course, so she could talk to all of the animals and tell me what they said.

Anyway, when the knock came on the back door, the first thing I did was go to the front window and look out. I was still wound tight as a guitar string, but instead of being scared I was in full-bore attack mode. It was like my minute with Donnie had flipped a switch or something. But the driveway and the curb were empty. So I told Emma to sit tight, and I went out through the kitchen to the pantry. That girl Shelley, the one I'd carried in from the rain, was standing outside the door.

I didn't know whether to open the door or not. If it had been one of the McClaine boys I might have ripped the door off the hinge to get at him, but seeing her instead, and knowing that she had already taken at least one beating because of me, it took all the starch out of me. I felt sleepy and tired all of a sudden and I wanted to walk away from her and everything she represented. It wasn't like I thought the whole mess was going to miraculously disappear. I knew it wouldn't. But I didn't want to have to deal with it anymore.

I opened the wood door and stood there looking at her through the screen.

She said, "I just came to talk."

"We have nothing to say to each other."

That was when Phil came out around the corner and slid in front of her. His brother was right behind him.

Phil said, "We have a lot to say to each other. And we're going to say it now."

I stepped back to close the door but then Phil punched his fist through the screen and shoved the door back against my hand. "You think a door's going to keep us out?" he said.

Every muscle in my body went tight and hard. All I wanted was to kick open that screen door and start swinging. But a part of me knew better—knew I couldn't take both of them empty-handed. And Bubby was grinning like he wanted me to do it. Like he was just waiting for a reason to pull out his knife or a gun.

I reached into my pocket then for my cell phone, but Phil yanked open the screen door and stepped in fast, shoving the wood door all the way open. His brother and Shelley were right behind him. Right away I'm calculating how fast I could run out to the garage and grab Pops' revolver out of the saddlebag.

He said, "Put the phone away. Unless you want Bubby to go see how little Emma's doing."

"You fucking touch my daughter—"

"And what?"

"I swear I'll fucking kill you."

"How can you do that when you're already going to be dead?"

By now that fat Neanderthal Bubby was standing right up there beside Phil, both of them with shit-eating grins on their faces. They'd pushed me back till I was up against the dryer. I figured I could probably take Phil, but both of them together? And me with bruised ribs and no room for moving around? That's when all the air went out of me.

So I said, "I've been planning all along to give it back to you."

"I wouldn't think it would take much planning."

"You threatened my family. That pissed me off."

"I'm sorry about that, Russell." He put a hand on my shoulder, which made me stiffen and jerk away. "No hard feelings, okay? Hand over what doesn't belong to you, and you can go right back to babysitting."

That was when I knew for sure that Donnie was messed up with them somehow. Who else could've known Emma wasn't in daycare? Cindy might've told some people at the bank, but how many of them would know the McClaines? No, it was Donnie for sure. Maybe Janice too.

I told him, "I don't have it here."

"Where do you have it?"

"Nowhere I can get it till tonight. After Cindy gets home."

"Then I guess we need to work out some details," he said.

I heard little feet on the kitchen linoleum then, so I called out, "Stay there, honey. Go back in the living room, okay?"

Bubby turned to her and said, "Hey, baby girl. You having a tea party today?"

"That was yesterday," she said.

"I'm sorry I missed it." And now he went into the kitchen and toward her. "How about showing me what you're doing today?"

I grabbed Phil by the shirtfront then and got up close in his face. He kept grinning. "You get him the fuck away from her *now*."

"I'll go," Shelley said. She went into the kitchen then and whispered something to Emma. "Okay!" Emma said.

Pretty soon Bubby came back out into the pantry. He said, "They're going to play hide-and-seek."

"See?" Phil asked. "Nothing to worry about. Shelley's good with kids."

I was breathing hard. Everything around me was in gray, everything but those brothers. "I can bring it to you tomorrow night," I said. "But then that's the end of it. You leave my family alone."

They kept looking at me. Neither of them was grinning now.

I said, "I made a mistake. I'm sorry. All I want now is to make things right and be done with this."

After ten seconds or so, Phil smiled again. Then he laid his hand on my shoulder and sort of pulled me toward the kitchen. "Let's negotiate. Out in the garage."

With him leading the way, and Bubby breathing down my neck, we went into the kitchen and then to the garage. The man had never been in my house before but he seemed to know it already. All I could think of was that fucking Donnie.

So we go out to the garage and Bubby closes the door behind us. Then he finds the light switch and flips it on. I keep walking until I'm up close to my bike.

Phil says, "Who else knows you took it?"

"Nobody," I say.

"Your wife?"

"Not even her."

Bubby says, "Keeping it all for yourself, huh?"

"My little girl was sick. I lost my job. I had no insurance, no money for a doctor."

"So that gives you the right to take our money?"

"I told you, I'm sorry I did it. I've been sorry every day since then."

Phil nodded and looked at his brother, who sort of shrugged, like he couldn't care less. Phil said, "You're going to have to take a beating, you know that, don't you? For fucking Shelley if nothing else."

"I never touched her! Except for carrying her in out of the rain after she fell on her back, I never laid a finger on her."

Bubby came up close to me then, shoved his big belly right up against me. "You're full of shit, you know that?"

I shoved him away hard, as hard as I could. It made enough room for me to spin around and make a grab for the saddlebag, but that was as far as I got. Phil slammed me facedown until I was bent over the bike seat, my hands jammed up underneath me. Next thing I knew Bubby was yanking me around and driving a fat fist into my chest, knocking me back so hard I fell on my ass on the floor. It was like he'd crushed my chest and collapsed my lungs, that's how it felt. I started gasping for air but couldn't suck any in.

He was moving toward me again when Phil told him, "Enough." Then Phil was kneeling down beside me. He grabbed me around the throat and squeezed so hard I heard myself groan, exactly like I'd done to Donnie the day before. Even with both my hands on his wrist I couldn't pull free. There wasn't any strength left in me.

"Tomorrow night," he said. "10:00 p.m."

I nodded as best I could while choking.

"You remember where you used to work?" he said. "The crushing plant?"

He let up on my throat a little, enough that I could swallow and cough. Then I told him, "Guards maybe."

"No guards. I already checked that out. You park behind the crusher building and wait for me inside. Capiche?"

I nodded again.

"You come alone. And you better bring every fucking dollar. If you don't, you'll be coming home to an empty house. Is that understood?"

I didn't answer right away because my mind was racing, trying to think of some way out of this, some way to get at the revolver. I'd already spent how much of the money? Hell, I couldn't even think straight, couldn't add any of it up. I kept trying to get my feet underneath me but all he had to do was yank me one way or the other and I'd lose my footing.

I guess he didn't like it that I wasn't answering so he let go for an instant, then threw me into a chokehold with his forearm locked up against my throat.

"You better understand," he said, and then clamped his forearm down hard. It wasn't long before everything even right in front of my face melted into darkness. I felt like I was turning into some kind of hot black tar, slipping away and oozing over the concrete floor. Then everything went quiet. Quiet and black and deep. And my body sort of evaporated away from me.

I have no idea how long I was out before I heard myself breathing again. Probably not long. But when I came to and got most of my senses back, I was alone. I got up and stumbled back inside the house and went straight to the living room, which was as empty as the pantry and the kitchen.

"Emma!" I called. "Emma, baby, where are you?"

She came out from behind the long drapes on the front window. "Where's the lady, Daddy?"

I scooped her up in my arms. "She had to go, I guess."

"She couldn't find me, could she? I won!"

"You won, baby."

"Can we play again?"

"Maybe later, okay? Let me hold you for a while."

*

I'd tried every way I could not to drag anybody else into this shit storm with me. By next morning I'd decided the best thing to do was to pack up what money there was left, which was most but not all of it, and hand it over to McClaine and promise to pay him back the rest in installments. If I had to take another beating, so be it. In one sense, I knew I deserved it. Then maybe life could get back to something like normal again, without me flinching at every sound and shadow.

If they ended up killing me, then all I'd have to say is that they'd better be smart about it. I'd remind them how many people knew about them harassing us. Hell, even the vice principal at Dani's school knew a little something about it. I'd tell Phil I left notes with three different people saying I had a late-night business meeting with him. And if he was really smart, he'd take me up on my offer of installment payments, because then he could collect interest on the debt.

I spent the first half of the afternoon convincing myself that my plan would work, then started worrying about how I was going to get out of the house that night without Cindy asking a bunch of questions. I wasn't all that sure I could even keep my nerves under control. Chances were ten to one she would see right through me.

I also spent some time convincing Emma that "the lady" who played hide-and-seek with her came with two guys interested in buying my bike. Cause I knew there was no way to keep Emma from telling Cindy about them being at the house. Emma hadn't seen but a glimpse of the two guys, if even that, so I was safe there. Shelley was the problem. Had been ever since I first laid eyes on her.

And yep, Cindy and Dani came through the door a little after five, and there goes Emma gushing on and on about the pretty lady who came and played hide-and-seek with her and how Emma won because nobody but Daddy knew where she was hiding.

Of course Cindy looked at me and said, "What lady?"

"I think she was the girlfriend of this young guy who stopped by to ask about the bike. Him and his father, I think."

"Ask what?"

"He heard I might be looking to sell it."

"Where would he hear that?"

"I mentioned it to a couple people at the picnic on Labor Day."

"I thought we talked about that. How would you get to work in the future?"

"I know. I wasn't thinking when I mentioned it at the picnic. I guess I was sort of panicking about not having a job and all."

"Did they make an offer on the bike?"

"Yeah but it was way too low. Plus the guy had never ridden a bike before. I told him he needed to start out on something smaller. Like a five hundred maybe. Get some experience, you know? You don't start out on an eight-hundred-pound bike unless it comes equipped with training wheels."

"You told him that?" she said.

"His father laughed and shook my hand for it. Said he'd been telling the boy the same thing."

Cindy smiled at that, so I knew it was a good time to change the subject. I said to Emma, "Tell Mommy what we made for dinner."

"Pasgetti!" Emma said.

"We smelled it in the garage," Dani said.

"The sauce is ready, but I have to put the pasta in and toast the garlic bread," I said.

"A salad?"

"You bet."

And that was how I got over the first hurdle. I still had to get out of the house later, and I still had to come back home alive.

I know you know what it's like to come back home again after a deployment, Spence. I worked a long time after the desert to get my tender feelings back. And now they were killing me. All that afternoon, every time I looked at Emma I'd have to fight back the tears. Then again while all of us were sitting there having supper together. I kept looking at all of them and wondering, what if this is the last time I ever spend with you? Then I'd look at Cindy's belly, what I could see of it above the table, and think about the tiny little baby in there, and wonder, will I ever get a chance to hold you?

I knew I had to man up and face the music, Spence, but Jesus I was feeling weak. All I really wanted was to gather my girls around me and pull up the covers and shut out the world.

And then I heard your voice. I swear I did. After dinner I'd sent the girls into the living room, so I was out in the kitchen alone, loading up the dishwasher and wiping off the counters. And that's when I heard you. *Brothers stand together*, you said. *You find yourself in a shit storm, you call on your brother.*

I actually turned around and looked, because it sounded like you were right there beside me. I know I didn't imagine it. And I knew exactly what you meant. It was probably the clearest thought I'd had all day. Before every mission you said the exact same thing to us. We weren't in it alone, that's what you were telling us. No matter how afraid and alone we felt, we had our brothers there with us. "Time to do the dance," you always said. The dance with Death. The one dance we all danced together.

Of course I would've called you, Spence, if you'd been here to call. And you would've come running, I know that too. But only one other name came to me. I kept asking myself, who else? Who else do I know around here who's been where we've been and done what we've done? And I kept coming back to the same one man. The one man I didn't want to call.

He'd been through it too. A different place and a different time, but it was still the same dance, wasn't it? The one only soldiers know.

Need your help, I texted Pops. *Call me a little before nine and ask me to come see you. Will explain when I get there.*

*

It started thundering around eight that night. Deep, rolling growls that kept getting closer and closer, then finally exploding into booms that made the girls squeal and pull the covers over their heads. I sat there on the edge of Dani's bed, reading to them and making jokes about the thunder so they wouldn't be too scared. I could hear Cindy out in the kitchen gathering up the candles and flashlights the way she always did when a storm hit at night.

After I got the girls tucked in I sat out on the couch with Cindy, just sitting there with my arm around her, both of us jumping every time lightning cracked and lit up the windows. When Pops' call came we both jumped again. But by that time the thunder and lightning had given me an idea.

"I gotta go spend some time with Pops," I told Cindy after I tucked the phone back in my pocket.

And it was like she had already read my mind. "It's Vietnam again, isn't it?" she said.

"He didn't say as much but . . . yeah. That's probably what it is."

"Bring him back here if you want," she said.

"Yeah, I think he probably wouldn't want you or the girls to see him that way. You be okay for a few hours?"

She nodded. "I'm awfully glad you got over yours," she said. "You have, right?"

"For the most part," I said.

We hugged for a minute in the kitchen, then I went out to the garage. She watched me driving away. I could picture her walking through the house then, making sure all the doors and windows were locked, probably taking a cover off the bed so she could sit bundled up on the couch with her phone, the flashlights, and a big-ass butcher knife lined up on the coffee table.

*

The first thing Pops said to me was, "It's about those McClaine boys, isn't it?" He was fully dressed and ready to go, and he didn't even know yet what was waiting for us. Still tough as nails after all these years. I filled him in on everything that had happened that week, and he kept getting madder and madder. "Let's go," he finally said.

"Pops, I'm doing this alone. I'm only telling you this so that, I don't know, you can give me some advice or something. I felt like you should know about this in case things go bad for me."

What I was really hoping for was that he would have some kind of miracle solution to everything. He didn't.

"Things already went bad," he said, and then he walked right out of his little apartment and into the hallway. "Pull the door shut," he said.

I followed him to the front desk, where he signed himself out. "My son's taking me out for some Chinese food and fast women," he told the attendant. "Don't wait up for me."

She chuckled and gave me a wink. "Make sure you use a condom," she said.

As soon as we were in the truck, Pops said, "Where you keeping my .30-30? Is it at your place?"

"It's at your storage unit."

"Let's go then," he said.

"I already been there, Pops. To get the money in that shoebox." He looked down at it on the floor by his feet.

He gave it a little nudge with his foot. "You say it's short?"

"I took some out to pay my ER bill."

"Why in the world didn't you come to me for a loan?"

"I should've, I know. I didn't want you to know I was in trouble."

"Let's find us an ATM then."

"It won't be enough, Pops. There's a limit on how much you can take out in one day."

He sat there thinking for a minute. Gave the shoebox another nudge. "Money's not all they're going to be looking for tonight."

"I know that," I said.

He looked at me then—a long, hard look. "Take me to the storage unit. We're not meeting those fellas unarmed."

"I already told you, Pops. I don't want you getting hurt. You can wait for me out in the truck while I deal with them."

He wasn't going to hear it. "You can get yourself that old revolver of mine too. You'll need something you can keep out of sight."

I pointed at the glove box. "It's in there."

He opened the glove box, took out the .22 and checked to see it was fully loaded. "You bring extra ammo?"

"I forgot and left it at home."

He shook his head, and I knew he was right. I'd stopped thinking straight the moment I decided to go back to that damn shower stall. And tonight I hadn't planned anything beyond me either walking back out of the crusher building, or crawling out all busted up, or trying to take both of the McClaines down with me before I bled out on the concrete floor.

I should've been more like you, Spence, the way you always laid out all the possibilities before a mission, the way you looked at all the angles. "This is what's probably going to happen," you'd say, and then you'd tell us how to play it out. But then you'd run through all the other possibles too, and tell us what to do in every case, Scenarios A, B, C and D. Most likely to least likely. High percentage to low.

Me, I'd only been thinking what I was going to do. What I should've been thinking was what the McClaines were most likely to do. Scenario A, B and C at least. Then how I could keep them from doing any of it in the first place. Or how I'd better react when they actually did it.

That's the way Pops was thinking. He tapped his finger against the face of the dash clock. 9:17. "Quit driving like an old lady and step on it," he said. "You think they'll come waltzing in at ten on the button? They're going to be early. They're going to assume you weren't stupid enough to come alone, and they'll want to pick their own best spots in case they're right. So we got to be earlier. Now punch that fucking gas."

I drove as fast as I could without spinning out on the wet roads. Pops sat hunched forward, keeping his face close to the windshield like he was searching for something in every flash of lightning. The only other thing he said before we got to the storage unit was, "You need to replace those wipers. They're about as useful as tits on a rooster."

*

Pops had me douse the lights at the bottom of the hill leading up to the crushing plant. A heavy chain hung across the dirt road at a height of three feet or so, suspended between a couple of concrete poles. "Looks like the Chinese haven't changed it yet," I said. "It's only an S-hook on each end, hanging from an eyebolt."

Pops wound down the side window, but there wasn't much he could see by then. The rain was pounding down on the roof and against the windshield harder than ever. Just hearing each other talk was an effort.

I watched the rain sheeting off the glass with every swipe of the wiper blades, and that's when I realized something. The trouble got started in a rainstorm, and now it was going to end in a rainstorm. How it would end was still to be seen.

After getting his face soaked, Pops rolled the window up again. "It's impossible to tell if they're here already or not." He tapped the readout on the dash clock again: 9:43. "My guess is they are."

I said, "So I drive on up, go in through the open end of the building, and hand over the money. You stay in the truck, all right? And keep out of sight. If they come back out and I don't, wait till they're gone before coming in to check on me."

"Coming in to scrape you up off the floor, you mean." He rubbed a hand up and down against his cheek. Then he picked the revolver up off his lap and handed it to me. "Go ahead and take the chain down.

Wait for me to drive on through, then hook it up again. That way, if they aren't here yet, they might think we aren't either."

"What's this for?" I said, meaning the revolver.

"In case they're out there laying for you."

"Why would they do that, Pops?"

"Just take it, okay? Makes me feel better."

So I climbed out with the revolver in my hand. I unhooked one side of the chain, then stepped aside so Pops could drive on through. Thing is, he kept on going. He hit the gas and away the truck went, up the road, spraying me with mud as I stood there by the concrete pole with the chain in my hand, wondering what the hell he was doing.

It didn't take me long to figure it out. He knew the layout of the plant as good as I did. He knew how long it would take me to climb a hundred yards up that slippery road on foot. He knew he would have plenty of time to turn over the money and deal with whatever happened next. He wanted to keep me out of it. Wanted to make sure I got home again.

I went up that hill as fast as I could, but it wasn't easy going. I kept slipping and sliding in the mud, falling down and getting up and falling down again. Exactly like in some of the fucking nightmares I have, except in them I'm always trying to save one of the girls from something. This time it was Pops, and this time it was for real.

Up near the top when I could finally see the yard I got a surprise. All the machinery was gone. The conveyers, the feeder, the washer, even the big front loader. The yard was empty but for a couple piles of rock. All this time I had been figuring I had an advantage over the McClaines because I knew where everything was. Knew where to run for cover if I had to. Where to tell Pops to hide out if he had to run.

As far as I could tell, the truck was nowhere to be seen. Nor was any other vehicle. The long metal building where the cone crusher was had a row of narrow windows up near the high roof, and in the dark I could see a light moving around inside. So either Pops was in there with his flashlight, checking things out, or one or more of the McClaines was. So I sneaked up to the building as quiet as I could. What with my footsteps squishing the entire way, I was grateful for once for the thunder and pounding rain.

The feeling I had was the same as being on patrol, Spence. That same adrenaline rush like when you come to a house that needs to be searched and you've got no idea what's waiting on the other side of the door. Worrying about the guys on the stack team and wanting to be there with them when they go rushing into the unknown, but you're on perimeter security and need to keep your eyes focused on the other houses. And all this time you're waiting for the bullets to rip, or for an explosion to light up your world and knock you ass backward out of it.

I made my way around to the big open end where we'd drive the front loader in and out. Inching closer to it I could hear snatches of voices inside, so then I knew. I couldn't make anything out, what with the rain banging and echoing like birdshot against the metal roof, but voices meant Pops wasn't in there alone.

At the edge of the open bay I sank down on my knees, one hand in the mud, so that my head wasn't two feet off the ground, and peeked inside. They had Pops sitting up against an I-beam, facing the bay, with the McClaines standing there beside him, one on each side. The whole building was empty, with nothing but a few oil stains where all the equipment used to sit. Phil was facing me but looking down at Pops. Bubby was standing sideways behind Pops' right shoulder, no doubt keeping an eye on the two closed doors, one on the front of the building and one on the narrow end opposite me. The shoebox with the cash in it was at his feet.

I couldn't tell if Pops was hurt or not. But he was talking to Phil a mile a minute, I could see that much but couldn't make out what he was saying. With nothing but roof, I-beams, and the concrete floor, their voices sort of rolled around in there so that when they reached me it was just a kind of hum. Both Phil and Bubby were holding chrome handguns. Nine mils, it looked like. The light was coming from a little battery-operated lantern set up in front of Pops.

Pops' mouth kept working, with him looking up at Phil all the while. Probably trying to convince him he had come alone. Probably something like, "If I'm not back in my bed by midnight, one of my poker buddies is gonna pass the news on to every last remaining member of Company 271, along with names and photos of you two and Shelley and even that shit-ugly dog of yours."

Pops could spin some real stories when he wanted to. Mostly he did it as a joke, but I figured he was doing it in there so as to alert me he wasn't alone. Whatever his reasons, those McClaine boys didn't seem to care much. They stood there watching and waiting. They knew I had to come in sooner or later.

I kept peeking into the building, never for more than a second or two at a time, trying to figure out my next move, my knees and one hand sinking into the mud. Finally I told myself to get up and do something. Should I walk in with the revolver popping, first shot toward Bubby, then swinging a bit to fire over Pops' head at Phil? A .22 doesn't have a lot of stopping power, not unless it's used up close enough to leave a powder burn on the skull. So should I tuck the revolver in behind my back and walk inside with my hands in the air? Should I leave the revolver in the mud? I had no fucking idea at all.

I eased myself up and backed away from the opening and then worked my way back around the building, across the wide front, then to the narrow end close to the squat little cinderblock office building. I still had no idea what to do, just that I had to get closer if I was going to do any good. If I tried to rush them, even from behind, they would have a clear shot at me, not to mention at Pops. And I doubted very much that Pops had convinced them of anything. It was me they wanted, and sooner or later they were going to have me. Even if I walked away tonight, that wouldn't be the end of it. Would they have Shelley charge me with rape? Would they keep harassing us through the girls, so that there'd be no end to this hell? And what about the missing money? How would I ever pay that back?

I'd never see the end of it. That's the only thing I managed to figure out for sure while sneaking around the building in the mud and the rain. It's like the war, Spence, you know? It never lets you be. Even after you come home, buy a nice little house, try to fit in and live a decent life, it's always there with you, isn't it?

I started telling myself I could end it all right then and there. As if the McClaines were some kind of weird extension of Iraq. As if it was all the same fucking war.

On the narrow end of the building, I eased open the metal door a foot or so, then slammed it shut as hard as I could. While the boom was still echoing inside, I raced around to the identical door at the front, grabbed it, pulled it open, and banged it shut.

This time a bullet came ripping through the door. But I was already running back to the narrow end. I figured I had them off balance now. Counting the bay, there were three entrances: Where would I appear next? They couldn't keep their eyes on all three entrances at the same time, and I was hoping either Phil or Bubby would be watching the open bay, and the other one would be watching the door he'd just now put a bullet through.

I yanked the other door open, dropped down low and fired into the nearest body, which was Bubby's. I caught him in the ribs, which left him staggering to his right. Phil was facing the front door but immediately spun toward me. Luckily Bubby was between him and me now, so Phil's first shot went wide. I put another bullet into Bubby, who crumpled to his knees, and then went down onto his hands as well, with blood spurting out of his chest and onto the concrete floor.

With Bubby down, Phil and I had open shots at each other, except that now Phil slid over for some cover behind Pops and the I-beam. But instead of shooting at me, Phil hunkered down low and put his gun to Pops' head and said something to him. But what Phil didn't know about

Pops was that this old man could still walk so fast that his grandson couldn't keep up with him. This old man could shovel snow for three hours without a pause, long after his grandson petered out and had to take a break. This old man had been put together with baling wire and fence posts, and he loved me more than anything else in the world.

That old man balled up a fist and drove it hard against the inside of Phil's knee, and then, like a tenth of a second later, leaned sideways and pushed his head and shoulders between Phil's legs, driving him into the open. I aimed for his head but missed, and put the next one in his shoulder. His gun arm went limp and he went down onto one knee while trying to switch the gun into his left hand. But Pops made a grab for it, twisted hard, and wrenched the gun free. He stood up, breathing fast and standing a little bit crooked, and aimed that chrome pistol at McClaine's head. But McClaine wasn't going anywhere.

"Go get your truck and pull it inside here," Pops called to me. "It's parked on the other side of the office." He handed me the 9 mm. "Take this," he said. "It's got more shots left. I'll take the revolver."

I said, "What do I need more shots for?"

"You don't know who else is out there," he said. "They might not've come alone."

So I switched weapons with him and went running out into the rain. As soon as the rain hit me I started to shake and felt like I couldn't get any air into my lungs. I was cold as hell all of a sudden, shivering like a drenched cat. McClaine's Avalon was parked behind the office too, but I had all I could think about trying not to freak out while I climbed into the truck and drove back to the bay entrance.

Pops was waiting there for me, and waved me to a stop before I turned inside. I put down the window and looked out. "I changed my mind," he said, and handed me a set of keys. "Leave the truck here and bring the car in instead."

He didn't want any blood in my vehicle. Didn't want my muddy tread marks on the concrete. But what were we going to do with the

McClaines? I was pretty sure Bubby was done for, but Phil only had a shoulder wound.

Anyway, I climbed out of the truck and hustled back toward the Avalon, hoping Pops had a plan of some kind. I had a strange feeling running through the rain and the dark, I'm not sure how to describe it. My body felt heavy, but I was also tingling all over, and my movements all seemed to be in slow motion, but not hard or difficult, just kind of dreamlike.

Then I unlocked the Avalon and climbed inside. It smelled like cigarette smoke and air freshener. As soon as I turned the ignition, the music came on. McClaine had Sirius Radio, and it was tuned to a classic rock station. That guy with the really high voice, Christopher Cross, he was singing about sailing away somewhere. It was all just too surreal. I wanted to break out laughing but I also couldn't stop shivering.

I heard what sounded like a single muted pop a couple seconds before the Avalon turned the corner into the building. My breath caught and I wondered if Pops was okay, but then I turned the car into the bay and there he was in the headlights, holding the revolver and looking down at Phil McClaine laying belly-down on the floor.

I pulled up to within ten feet of them, put the car in park and then felt like I couldn't move. If I moved, all of that mess in front of me would be real.

Pops came walking toward me then and laid the revolver on the hood. Then he pulled off his T-shirt and motioned for me to put down the window. I did, and he handed me his shirt. His body was white and his chest sunken. He looked so small and weak to me then, and he was walking sort of lopsided, holding his left shoulder higher than the other one.

"Wipe the steering wheel, the keys, anything else you touched. Leave the keys in the ignition."

I did what he told me, then climbed out. I couldn't help staring down at Phil and the puddle of blood around his head. Pops struggled to pull his shirt back on. "You know this is the only way it could have ended good for you," he said.

"I didn't expect it to end good."

"I did," he said.

I kept standing there, feeling sort of like I wasn't even in my body anymore. Like the real me was over in the corner somewhere, watching it all.

Pops gathered up the box of money, then the revolver off the hood of the Avalon. With his foot he nudged the chrome pistol across the floor so it lay closer to Phil. "Let's go," he said.

"We're just going to leave them here?"

"They're a Chinese problem now, son. Let's go."

We walked out toward the bay door. I turned around to take a last look inside. And that's when I saw them. All those muddy footprints.

I bent over and pulled my shoelaces loose. Pops said, "What are you up to now?"

"Look inside."

He did, and it took him about five seconds to understand. "Good thinking," he said. He bent toward his own shoes, but then he winced and kind of moaned "Ahh" and put a hand up to his chest.

"What's wrong?"

"Nothing. A little pinch is all."

"Go get in the truck, Pops. I'll take care of this."

"Why not," he said. "I guess I wiped up after you a good many times when you were little, didn't I?"

"You always have. Go take a rest."

I pulled off my socks then, set my shoes around the outside corner and off the concrete, and held the socks in the rain till they were soaking wet. Then I went inside and crawled around on my hands and knees, smearing every one of my and Pops' prints into a pale brown circle. It wasn't a perfect job but perfect wasn't necessary. It was quick and it was enough.

I put my shoes on again and went back to the truck. Pops was sitting in the passenger seat, so I tossed my wet socks onto the floor, climbed in behind the wheel and started the engine. I needed the headlights to get back down the slippery road safely. Pops told me how the moment he'd pulled the truck up alongside the Avalon earlier, Phil McClaine was at his door with a gun pointed at his head. "If you'd kept the revolver like I wanted you to," I said.

He shook his head. "Could'ves and would'ves never accomplished a thing. We got it done. That's all that matters."

We were maybe ten yards from the bottom of the lane when a figure came out from the side darkness to unhook the chain.

"Who the fuck is that?" Pops said, squinting through the windshield.

"Donnie," I told him.

"Son of a bitch."

"What do I do?"

"Look at him grinning. He thinks it's a McClaine boy driving."

"Should I drive through?"

"Pull on up beside him." Pops laid the revolver atop his leg, ready to put a bullet through the window if he had to.

I did, then held the brake down. Donnie walked up to the window, grinning all the way. He had to get his face right up to the side window to recognize me through the film of rain. Then his grin disappeared, kind of twitching a little and fading away as sure as if the rain had washed it right off his face.

He turned back the way he had come, taking long strides at first, then breaking into a run. I drove out to the end of the lane and there was Bubby's pickup parked along the shoulder. Donnie hopped into the passenger side, and within seconds the pickup was squealing away.

"Better follow them," Pops said.

*

Following Donnie and the truck wasn't so much a follow as a chase. The moment the other pickup's driver saw my headlights turn their way, they floored it.

Pops sat up close to the windshield, still holding tight to the revolver. "This is no time to drive like your grandmother, son. Keep up."

The driver turned off the main road at the first left. After that we flew down black asphalt single lanes, squealing and sliding through turn after turn. Sometimes we lost sight of their taillights, then picked them up again and tried to close the distance. We were maybe four miles out in the country when the driver took a left turn too sharp, fishtailed and overcorrected. I saw the taillights turn over in a circle and a half before they both blinked out in pink puffs of glowing smoke.

"Pull over here," Pops said. We were maybe fifty feet back from the upside-down pickup truck. "Keep your headlights on. But if you see a vehicle coming up behind or toward you, kill the lights and lay down on the seat."

He sprung open the door and climbed out, taking the revolver with him. I watched him walking that fast short-legged walk of his, but there was something not right about it, something a little lopsided, almost as if he had to shove himself forward with every other step.

He went to the driver's side first, knelt down in the gravel and looked inside and then put his hand in. Then pulled it out again and walked around to the other side, which was in the grass over top of the drainage ditch.

He didn't even go the whole way up to the window, but stood there about three feet from it looking at something in the grass. Then he looked back at me. I thought about climbing out and calling to him, but before I could, here he comes back my way.

He comes right up to the window. "If I ask you to do something for me, Rusty, will you do it? One last thing, no questions asked?"

"Pops, what are you—?"

"Russell. One last thing. Last thing I will ever ask of you."

"There's nothing I wouldn't do for you. You know that."

"And there's nothing I wouldn't do for you. And do it gladly."

"I know."

"I want you to lay down on the seat now and not look up till I come back."

"Pops, no. I'm not going to do that."

"Goddamn it, son. One last thing, that's all I'm asking of you."

"Who was driving the truck?"

"Shelley."

"She's dead?"

He nodded.

"What about Donnie?"

"Whyn't you cut your lights, all right? Then wait here till I get back. Is that too much to ask?"

"Tell me why, Pops."

"Damn it, Russell. Do you love your children?"

"You know I do."

"You want to be able to look at their faces and not see anything except those beautiful smiles? Not see all the shit that's taking up all the space in your memory right now? Do you want that or not?"

"Of course I want that."

"Then cut your lights, son."

So I did.

Pops reached in and patted me on the shoulder. "I'll be right back. You lay down now and sit tight."

I leaned down on the seat with my face to the beat-up old leather. It was still warm from where Pops had been sitting. I laid there tense and waiting for a gunshot, but all I heard was the rain on the roof and hood.

Then his footsteps crunching back over the gravel. And then the side door popping open. "Sit up and start driving," he said.

He climbs in breathing hard, and I can see him wincing when he twists around to pull the door shut.

"Where's the revolver?" I asked.

"Don't worry about it."

"Pops, you can't leave it there."

"It's unregistered, son. Now get us the hell out of here."

*

On our way back through town, about ten minutes from his apartment, he had me pull to the curb about a block from a 7-Eleven. "I'll walk home from here," he said.

"It's still raining pretty good."

"I get a hot chocolate and a Slim Jim here every night. One for me and one for Margie at the front desk. Rain or no rain, it makes no difference to me."

"Yeah but at close to midnight? Without a hat or an umbrella or anything?"

"Anytime between ten and four. Old men don't sleep much. Don't pay much attention to the weather either. I expect you'll find that out yourself someday."

He reached for the door handle then, but I reached out too and put my hand on his arm. "Why were you walking like that?" I said.

"Like what?"

"Back at the wreck. And even before it. Like you're hurt or something."

"I don't know, Rusty. Arthritis, sciatica, Parkinson's—take your pick."

"Yeah but you didn't walk like that till tonight. It's even worse than when we left the plant."

"I'm getting older every minute—what can I say?"

"Donnie was still alive, wasn't he? What did you have to do?"

He looked up through the blurry windshield awhile, just sat there staring at the darkness and the watery neon lights. The rain kept drumming down and I realized suddenly how much I liked the sound of it. How grateful I was for the sound itself and the coolness of the air and the fact that Pops and I were sitting there together listening to it.

And I couldn't help myself, Spence, but I started crying. And I started shaking. And I kind of collapsed up against the steering wheel and felt these rolling bubbles of pain coming up from my chest and out with every sob.

This went on for maybe thirty seconds or so with Pops not saying a word. Then he leaned toward me and pulled me away from the steering wheel. He clamped my cheeks in those thick, rough hands of his. And he put his face close to mine.

"Cindy," he said.

"Dani," he said.

"Emma," he said. "And one more on the way." Then he looked at me and asked, "You need to hear those names again?"

"No, sir," I said. "I don't."

He gave me a little pat on the cheek and smiled at me. "Just go on about your business like nothing's happened," he told me. "We'll talk after all this blows over." Then he climbed out and walked his crooked walk straight up the sidewalk.

I let him get inside the store before I drove forward again. I drove real slow, barely moving, and watched him give a little wave to the guy behind the counter. Watched him cross over to the hot chocolate machine and put a cup under the spout. Watched the guy behind the counter talking what looked like a blue streak, and Pops standing there nodding and smiling with his back to him, watching his cup fill up to the brim.

Back home a little while later, I parked in the garage and used the remote to put the door down behind me. What I wanted was to just sit there awhile by myself. My clothes were soaked and I was shivering again despite having the heater on. But I knew that if I stayed in the garage too long, and if Cindy had heard me pulling in, she'd be out to check on me. So I grabbed up my wet socks and tiptoed inside as quiet as I could. In the kitchen I wrung my socks out over the sink, then went to the girls' bathroom, stripped down naked and towcled off. I stuffed my wet clothes in the girls' laundry hamper, tiptoed into my bedroom, and thank God Cindy was sound asleep. I slipped a drawer open, got out a pair of underwear and a T-shirt. Cindy didn't wake up till I was crawling in beside her.

"How's he doing?" she said.

For a moment my mind went blank and I didn't know who she was talking about. Then I said, "He's okay. Just needed some company for a while."

"That's good. Night, babe." She reached out to lay her arm across my chest. I was afraid she might feel how cold I was, but she didn't. She went right back to sleep.

*

I have a question for you, Spence.

Wherever you are these days, do you ever feel alone?

If you do, you know what an awful feeling it is. It's the absolute worst. I remember feeling it when my mother died, and for a long time afterward. Then one day I woke up happy to be with Pops and Gee, happy to have the life they were giving me, and after that I didn't feel alone anymore. And thought I never would again.

Lots of times in Iraq I felt it too. Despite the closeness of our unit, despite the friendship I felt with you, it was easy to feel alone over there too. At night in my cot. On patrol. In the latrine. First thing in the morning when I'd wake up to the heat and noise and remember where I was.

Then I came home to Pops and Gee, then Cindy and the girls, and suddenly it seemed like I didn't have the time to be lonely anymore. Except at night sometimes, like when I was dreaming I was awake and

155

the air was too hot to breathe and I thought I could hear somebody creeping around outside, looking for a way to pitch an IED inside.

Then things finally smoothed out for me around the time I got my degree. I never told anybody, not even Cindy, but that graduation meant a lot more to me than being out of college. It was a turning point, I guess. I walked across that stage, then down onto the floor, then outside into the cool spring air, and I felt like I was finally back. Like I had left all that awful loneliness behind.

But it's been pounding me a lot lately, and at the oddest of times. I'll be watching TV in the living room with Cindy and the girls, all of us snuggled up together so close we're half on top of each other, and out of nowhere it will hit me like a shock wave, how all alone I really am. It will be all I can do at those times to keep the tears out of my eyes. At times like those, all I want to do is crawl off into some dark corner and hide.

Does that make any sense at all, feeling so miserable for being alone that I want to hide from everybody? It makes no sense to me.

Back in Iraq when the loneliness got to me, there were always my brothers to turn to, you most of all, but even the ones I didn't particularly like. Even they were my brothers. We ate together, slept together, shit together, whined and moaned and bitched and sometimes even cried together. We were a fucking unit, you know?

I'm in another unit now but it's different. I'm the one the girls all look to. The one who's supposed to provide everything they need and keep them safe from all insurgent forces. I have to keep secrets from them. I have to hide my emotions sometimes. I have to sugarcoat all the ugliest crap going on outside our FOB. And I've got nobody but you to unload on.

Truth is, it's not a very satisfying communication when it only goes one way.

Which makes me realize how you must've felt back there. You didn't sugarcoat anything but you were the point we all turned around. You were the source of our faith and our strength. You held us together and kept us going. But who held you together?

I'm sorry, brother, if that responsibility ever made you feel as alone as I do now.

I wouldn't wish this feeling on anybody.

*

Is it possible to hate something you did, and to hate yourself for doing it, yet still be glad you did it?

*

Iradat Allah. I bet you remember that phrase, don't you? How many hundreds of times did we hear that? *Iradat Allah.* The will of God. Then they'd sit down in the dirt beside the bloody bodies and commence into wailing and tearing at their clothes.

It always seemed like some kind of contradiction to me. First acceptance, then grief. I don't know, maybe it's not a contradiction at all. Maybe it's the natural order of things.

What made me bring it up now is a dream I had just a few minutes ago. I'm still fucking shaking from it. Thing is, I can't remember if it really happened or not. I mean that guy on the bicycle, he was real, I know that much. I know you ordered him to stop and he didn't, and you told me to take him out, so I did. I *know* that happened. But a minute or two later, after we'd checked him over and found he wasn't carrying anything, just my bullet in his chest now. Was there really a little girl who came up to me then and took my hand and told me, "Iradat Allah"?

That part's not real, is it, Spence? How could that have happened?

It just seemed so fucking real is all. I mean I can still feel her hand slipping into mine. I can still see her eyes staring into mine.

And even if it is just a dream, aren't dreams supposed to mean something? On one hand she's sort of forgiving me by telling me what I did was God's will, right? But on the other hand, what does that say about God? How's that make Him any different from the assholes who sent us over there in the first place?

*

I want to go back to that night now, the night after that hour or so up at the plant with Pops. Cindy got a call from her mother. It must have been around three something. Of course when the phone rang I jumped like a cockroach hitting a hot skillet. Luckily Cindy's phone was on the table on her side of the bed, so she rolled over and grabbed it, and that's how she found out her father was dead. Janice wanted Cindy to come down to a funeral home where the bodies had been taken. All I heard though was, "Where is he?" Then, "All right. I'll be there as soon as I can."

She climbed out of bed, then said to me, "Cover up your eyes. I need to turn on the light."

"What's wrong?" I said.

She went to her closet and started pulling out clothes. "I'm not sure anything is."

"What do you mean?"

"Donnie was in an accident. In a truck with that woman Shelley. They're both dead."

I sat up. "What?"

"I need to go be with Mom. She's barely coherent."

"Why would Donnie be in a truck with Shelley?"

"I wouldn't put anything past him," she said.

After she had on her jeans and a shirt, she sat on the bed to put her shoes on.

"Where'd you leave the keys?" she said.

"On the hook. Where they always are."

"I'm probably going to have to stay with her all night."

"As long as it takes," I said.

Before she left she asked me, "So what do you think that was all about?"

"What?" I said.

"Him and her together in that truck?"

I tried to look as surprised as she was. "Whatever it was, I guess neither one of them can cause any more trouble for anybody."

"No but those other two can."

No they can't, I thought. But I didn't say anything out loud. I tried to think of something to say, but then I remembered something else more important.

"You might want to take a towel with you to dry off the seat in the truck," I said. "It might still be wet."

"Wet from what?" she said.

"I tripped outside after leaving Pops' place," I told her. "Was more or less soaked by the time I got back to the truck."

"Tripped over what? Did you get hurt?"

"My own stupid feet. Naw, I landed in the grass. Just glad it was too dark for anybody to have seen me."

I guess that answer satisfied her, because she gave me a nod, then a peck on the cheek, and she headed out and switched off the light.

That next day, the only thing in the paper was a story about the pickup overturned along the side of the road. Skid marks indicated the truck had been speeding when the driver lost control.

Cindy spent all that day with Janice. Called me a few times to say hello, and probably to get a breather from her mother's grief. Cindy, for her part, only wanted to know why I thought Donnie was in the truck with Shelley that night. Wanted to know what was going to happen next, what the McClaine brothers might be doing or thinking right now. Janice had told the police that Shelley had lived with the

McClaines, so now the police were trying to locate Phil and Bubby, but so far they were still whereabouts unknown.

It wasn't until middle of the morning on Monday that Cindy started breathing easier. She called me from work to tell me everybody was talking about the McClaines being found up at the crushing plant. "Both dead," she whispered into the phone. "Shot to death. Can you believe that?"

"I suppose anything's possible," I said.

Apparently the Chinese had showed up Monday morning to do whatever they were doing up there, found the bodies, called the police. Back at the plant Pops had said Phil and Bubby were the Chinese's problem now, so I knew we were both hoping the Chinese would clean up the mess themselves, but apparently they intended to be good citizens about it.

By the end of the day customers were coming into the bank talking about the revolver found under Donnie's body at the wreck. The police hadn't mentioned it when the first news report came out, but now that Phil and Bubby had turned up, the township police turned everything over to the state boys, and they sent the revolver and recovered bullets off to be tested. According to Cindy, who had been hearing about it all day long from her customers and other tellers, a lot of people in town felt pretty good about the whole thing. Apparently we weren't the only people the McClaines and Donnie rubbed the wrong way.

"I think Mom's the only one feeling bad," Cindy told me.

"How about you?" I asked.

"What do you think?"

"Even so . . ."

"Even so what?"

"He's your father, that's all."

"That's only a word, Russell. Kind of an honorary title. Some men live up to it, other men don't."

Me, I kept holding my breath for the next couple days.

On Friday I started breathing again too. That was the day the ballistics report came out in the paper. All the evidence pointed to some kind of disagreement between the McClaine brothers and Donnie and Shelley. Most people figured drugs were involved. Others believed that Donnie was banging Shelley, and the McClaine boys found out about it. Somehow Donnie had gotten the upper hand in the crushing plant, and put an end to the disagreement with an unregistered .22 revolver. When Donnie and Shelley were fleeing the scene, driving too fast for conditions, poetic justice stepped in and had its say.

Of course there were other people who wanted to lay the blame on the Chinese somehow, like maybe they'd bought the crushing plant as a front for importing opium and heroin, or for setting up a mega-meth lab with Phil and Bubby handling the distribution.

I didn't care what crazy theories people came up with. The more, the better. As long as the police never looked in my direction or Pops'. I knew I'd be on pins and needles for a while until the case was officially closed, but nervousness was a small price to pay for all the trouble I'd caused.

Later that same afternoon I talked to Pops for the first time all week. I guess he'd read the paper too, and felt like it was time to get in touch again.

He called and said, "You doing okay?"

"Better now," I told him. "You?"

"Grateful for every breath I take," he said. "How are those little darlin's of mine?"

*

That same night when Cindy came home, she was looking at me kind of differently, I thought. All through dinner it was like she was sneaking glances at me. Usually when she and I do the dishes together, the girls will sit at the table, coloring or drawing or something. This time Cindy let them watch TV in the living room.

So I'm scraping the dishes over the disposal, then I hand them to Cindy and she rinses them clean and puts them in the dishwasher. She looks over her shoulder to make sure one of the girls isn't standing in the doorway, and then she says, "What do you think about what the police are saying?"

"What do you mean?" I said.

"That Donnie and Shelley did it."

"The McClaines, you mean?"

"I can't see it," she says. "I don't know what she was like, but I know Donnie, and I know he was never anything but a lying sneak and coward."

"Thing is, the bullets match the gun found underneath him."

She stared out the kitchen window and shook her head. "It doesn't make any sense. Why would the four of them get together up at that empty plant?"

"Maybe they were meeting somebody there. Most likely some kind of drug deal."

"There'd be evidence of that, wouldn't there?"

"It rained pretty hard all that night."

"Not inside it didn't."

"I only know what you told me and what I read in the papers."

She put the last of the silverware into the dishwasher, put in the gel, and set the dishwasher to running. I used a wet cloth to wipe down the table and counters.

"The real mystery," she says, "is why that girl would be with Donnie in the first place. Let's say it was them against the McClaines for some reason. Why? Why would she side with that piece of crap about anything?"

"Babe, there's no telling why people do what they do."

"There's absolutely no good reason for her to be with him."

"I didn't say it had to be a good reason. I mean, look at your mother. She took him back in a minute."

She didn't say anything more for a while. Then it was, "You've already wiped that table clean three times, Russell."

So I came back to the sink, rinsed out the cloth, wrung it dry, and draped it over the basin divider. I could feel her eyes on me the entire time. So finally I forced myself to turn around and face her and smile.

She said, "I never asked you how Pops was that night."

"Good," I said. "He was good. He was restless for a while. Needed somebody to distract him from his thoughts."

"What time was it when you got back?"

"It wasn't that late. Eleven thirty maybe?"

"You must've been awfully quiet getting into bed."

"You woke up for a minute," I told her. "You asked how Pops was doing."

"Did I? I don't remember that at all."

"You were barely awake," I said.

She nodded. "So that was it then? You went to his place for a couple hours, sat and talked, watched TV?"

"That's about it. Oh, I did drive him down to the convenience store before I came home. He usually walks but it was still raining pretty good. Turns out he can't make it through a night without his hot chocolate and a Slim Jim."

She wrinkled up her nose. "Those meat sticks are nasty."

I put my hand on the side of her face. "So is the interrogation over?"

"Why would you call it an interrogation?"

"That's what it felt like."

"Talking to your wife feels like an interrogation to you?"

"Baby," I said. But there wasn't anything more to say. Nothing halfway smart anyway. So I leaned over and kissed her on the forehead.

She surprised me by wrapping her arms around my waist and holding me there.

"The important thing," she said, "is that we're all okay now."

"Better than okay," I said.

"And the next time you see a naked girl?"

"It's going to be you."

"And the time after that?"

"You, you, and only you forever. No, wait. Newborn babies don't count, do they?"

"This one's going to be a boy," she said.

"We don't know that for sure."

"If it's not, I'm sending it back."

"Like heck you will."

And after that we held each other for a while. And that's the last we've ever talked about it.

*

I don't remember if I ever told you about my time in boot with this guy named Regis. Big mean tatted-up black guy who claimed he'd spent two years in prison for beating his brother to a pulp over a slice of pie or some such thing. Everybody in the barracks was scared to death of him. During the day he was all "Yes, Drill Sergeant! No, Drill Sergeant!" Always crushing every exercise and physical test, even marksmanship. So he was the platoon's golden boy, you know? From Day One the DIs were all but drooling over him. So of course they made him Squad Leader.

But he was different in the barracks at night. With no NCOs watching us every second, he was like some kind of marauding beast. I saw him put guys in a headlock until their eyes rolled up in their heads. The man was a terror, just like every clichéd character in every boot camp movie ever made. I guess his kind became a cliché because it's the truth. There's always one of them when you throw a bunch of guys together. I mean I've seen it before, though never to the extent of Regis. It was like living with a psycho in our midst. You never knew what he was going to do or who he'd do it to. You only prayed it wouldn't be you. That first week he probably knocked every one of us on our asses at least once, and always for something trivial, just because he felt like it.

The worst of it was what he did to a guy named Stewart. And Stewart wasn't a little guy either. He was a solid six feet tall, but kind of an egghead, I guess, sort of awkward and stiff, with a confused look in his eyes behind those ugly birth-control glasses the Army gives out. He was always talking about Harry Potter and stuff like that, things like alchemy and the philosopher's stone and subjects most of us didn't understand and didn't care to. Personally I never minded listening to him, because I was always ready to learn things I didn't know anything about, but sometimes even I had to call information overload and put him on hold awhile.

What Stewart was doing in the Army, I have no idea. All we could figure is he was such a social misfit that his old man must have sent him away to get toughened up. Thing is, I doubt his old man ever envisioned somebody like Regis as a bunkmate.

The abuse started maybe the third, fourth night of Red Phase. Not all of us heard it happening, but enough that that next day a bunch of us were comparing notes first chance we got. Not long after lights out Regis climbed into Stewart's bunk with him. What woke me was the crack of a slap. Stewart's bunk was only two away from mine, so that slap yanked me out of a deep sleep and had me sitting up and listening, trying to figure out what was going on. There was a lot of whispering and whimpering then, Regis' deep voice and Stewart's higher, terrified one.

What happened after that was pretty clear, what with Stewart gagging and whimpering and Regis' muttered threats.

The rest of us kept telling each other we needed to do something about it. I mean there were eighteen of us and only one Regis. But all we did was talk and whisper like a bunch of schoolgirls. Nobody wanted Regis turning on him instead.

This went on two or three nights a week. Regis must have memorized the Fire Guards' routine, because he was fast and slick and was always back in his own bunk when necessary. We all started avoiding both of them as much as possible, Stewart as well as Regis. That's something I could never figure out. It was almost like we blamed Stewart too, or were terrified of catching his bad luck. Or maybe we were just too afraid to be kind to him. I think about it now and I just want to throw up, that's how disgusted with myself I still am.

The only thing the rest of us did was agree to give Regis the lowest rating on evals. And we put the reason for the rating in the comment section. I don't know exactly how many of us actually did it, but enough that the DI and platoon sergeant interviewed both Regis and Stewart the next day. Neither of them even came back to clean out their lockers, not until the rest of us were out on the firing range.

After that the DI was tougher than ever on us. Like we were responsible for it happening in the first place, which I guess maybe we were. By graduation the rumor was going around that Regis had been transferred to another platoon, but Stewart got sent home on a medical discharge, though we all knew that was BS. I guess the Army wasn't willing to get rid of a killing machine with as much potential as Regis. Figured they'd just redirect his energies to more effective mayhem. The guy's probably an LT by now.

For some reason I feel like I needed you to know about this. Don't ask me why. You always seemed to like me for some reason, which I could never understand, a bright guy like you. Anyway, now you know. I never deserved a minute of your friendship.

I wonder what ever happened to Stewart. I could probably find out, but I'm sort of afraid to go looking. Once a coward, always a coward.

*

You always told us every time something bad happened, whether to us or by us, you always told us to not think about it. Try not to think about it, you said. But you thought about it, Spence. I know you did. The way I'd catch you looking at us sometimes, that sadness in your eyes like you knew something we didn't. Thing is, we knew it too. Shame. Grief. Fear. Disgust. There wasn't one of us over there who didn't know it and feel it every single day.

Thing is, they shave our heads and dress us in the same clothes and try to make us all look alike—hood rats and farm boys and poor white trash and everything else we were before they threw us all together. Then they drill us and teach us to shoot and fight and they do their damnedest to make us despise the enemy. They program us like machines so we'll use our weapons like the voice for our fear and anger and hatred, the only voice they let us have. The only one that will get us a word or two of congratulations from the company commander.

But deep down we're all still men. Boys, really. Deep down we all miss our homes and families and just want to get back to them in one piece. We all just want to feel loved and safe again, want to sit at the table with people glad to be with us, people who don't hate us because of the uniforms we wear, people who don't want to kill us.

And when some of us do come back in one piece, and we take off the uniforms and let our hair grow out, and we try to look like we were never in those places and never did what we know we did, deep down there's a poison in our blood that will never go away. More than ever now we just want to be loved and safe but there's always a dirtiness inside us. It won't wash out and the more we try to not think about it, we only think about it more.

That's what they really did to us, Spence. Every single one of us. Every war they've ever made us fight. They start by shaving our heads, but it's our souls they destroy.

*

For quite a while now I haven't been sure I'm going to be able to hold myself together. I keep thinking about what a good little boy I used to be, never getting into any real kind of trouble, doing everything Mom and Gee and Pops asked me to do. Growing up right with Jesus, as Gee used to say. And now the things I've done since then. Most days I can't even look at myself in the mirror.

It's getting a little better lately, though. For one thing, I keep getting busier and busier, and it's good to have stuff to focus on. I got that job at Lowe's after all. The manager called me out of the blue, said he'd run through all the other applicants and not one of them stacked up very well against me. I'd only been there a month and they offered to send me to North Carolina for their management training program.

Cindy's belly keeps growing, of course, which means I spend more and more time helping out with the chores when I'm at home. And having a girl in first grade—who'd have thought a first grader could be involved in so many activities? I can't imagine what it will be like when she hits junior high.

Pops and I still talk on the phone a couple times a week, not saying anything we shouldn't, only asking "How you feeling today?" and stuff like that. I brought up the way he was behaving the night of Shelley and Donnie's wreck, the way he'd been walking lopsided and mentioned he'd had a little pinch in his chest, but he wouldn't talk much about it. "Getting old," was as close as he'd come to admitting something was wrong with him. "Getting older every day."

Last week I tried to get him to go to a thing Dani was having at school, a little poem recital thing her teacher set up, but he said he was down with a bug and wanted to stay close to the toilet. Dani recited a poem called "The Caterpillar" that she'd been practicing at home all week long. I even know it by heart now too from listening to her practice. She did so good at the recital. Both Cindy and me had tears in our eyes watching her. Isn't that silly, Spence? To cry over a children's poem? I still tear up every time I look at the photos I took on my phone.

Plus sometimes I look at Dani or Emma or even Cindy while she's sleeping, and when I do, those last two lines of the poem are what I hear in my head.

> Spin and die,
> To live again a butterfly.

I hate the first of those lines, but I love the second one, and for the life of me I can't figure out why the poet put those two lines together like that. Especially in a children's poem. I mean Jesus, Spence. I want all my babies to be butterflies. But I can't bear the thought of any of them having to die first.

But here's the thing: until I heard that poem, I never thought the caterpillar really dies. I always figured he went into his cocoon and started changing, growing wings and legs and antennae and all, and of course thinning down that fat green body of his, but actually dying? And the more I thought about it, the less sense it made that the caterpillar would die and out would come a full-blown butterfly. Right? So I looked it up. And the truth of the matter is a whole lot weirder. The caterpillar *disintegrates*. Literally. It turns into a kind of caterpillar soup. Nothing left but a few random cells. And out of those cells comes the butterfly. Is that magical or what? Magical and terrifying all at the same time.

Anyway, overall, back to me and the family. I guess things couldn't have turned out any better for us. Except that when things get good like they are now, I know it's time to be ready for something bad to happen. That's pretty much the way life is set up to work, isn't it? You gain, you lose. You win, you fail. You spin, you die. Maybe too you liquefy and start yourself all over again as a butterfly, but maybe you're turned into a moth instead. And maybe something eats you before you ever get a chance to spread your wings.

*

I need to tell you about what happened one nice afternoon back in the third week of October, one of those Indian summer afternoons when the temperature is back up near eighty and the sky is so clear and blue. After I had come in from mowing the yard for what I guessed would be the last time that year, I found Cindy sitting there at the kitchen table with nothing in front of her and nothing in the stove or even thawing out on the counter. I got a glass of water and sat down across from her. "Everything okay?" I said.

She smiled like she'd been far away somewhere in her mind and wasn't all that happy about coming back but knew she had to. She said, "I think we could all use a night out, don't you?"

So everybody got a bath or a shower and then we picked up Pops and drove to this seafood house out by the mall. There was a parking space near the door, right beside one of those handicap spots with a shiny clean van in it, but when I went to pull into the space Dani said, "Not there, Daddy. What if there's somebody with the van who's in a wheelchair? There won't be enough room to get the wheelchair in and out."

Cindy looked at me and smiled and I sort of knew what she was thinking. *That's some girl we've got, isn't it, Russell?* So I found us another spot, and we all went inside, and darned if we didn't get seated not six feet from a table with a guy in a wheelchair. He looked to be at least ninety years old or more, this wizened little guy who didn't even have the strength to hold his head up. His wife was all dolled up in a sparkly dress and pearls, and she was enjoying her lobster bowl without hardly even looking at the old guy beside her, who I'm guessing was her husband. Sitting on the other side of the old guy was some young burly dude feeding the old guy his seafood bisque. The young dude would spoon up some bisque, then drain off the liquid and lay any chunks of seafood on his own plate, do this four or five times then go back to the bowl for some broth, which he would feed to the old guy. Half of it would run out of the old guy's mouth, so the young dude would dab a napkin at it. It was that over and over again—pick out the chunks, spoon up some broth, feed the old guy, dab up the dribble.

Of course Cindy told the girls to quit staring, but none of us could keep our eyes off them, including Pops. I don't think he'd said a word since we came into the place, and now he was sitting there like he was hypnotized by the old guy's face. And then I sort of got hypnotized by watching Pops watch the old guy, because I swear I could tell what Pops was thinking. He was thinking, all that money . . . a wife who must've been a beauty in her day . . . a fancy van and a fancy wheelchair and a personal attendant . . . and what good is any of it doing the guy?

And then Pops turned his head all of a sudden like he knew I was watching him, and there's no way he couldn't have seen what was in my eyes, and we had this moment, you know? This moment when he knew that I knew, and vice versa.

Fortunately the salads came then and kind of broke up what we were all feeling, and then we had our dinner and talked and laughed a little but there was always something hanging in the air that made us want to keep our voices low and filled us with a sad kind of tenderness for each other.

It was about a week after that Sunday, six days to be exact, when Pops called me in the morning and asked if I could get away for a few hours in the afternoon. All he would tell me was that he wanted me to drive him somewhere. "You can tell Cindy I'll have you back in time for supper," he said.

So I pick him up and he still won't tell me where we're going. "Head north," he told me.

"Anywhere in particular?"

"Straight up 62 North. It will take us a while to get there."

I noticed right away that Pops wasn't his usual self. A lot quieter, for one thing. But there was a stillness to him too that he didn't usually have. I think I told you before about how fidgety and restless he always used to be, always having to do something with his hands, whether it was cleaning his nails or tinkering with an old toaster or fixing some crack in the plaster that only he had ever noticed.

So we're riding along, and I'm giving him his quiet time and enjoying the fall leaves and all, when he comes out and asks if I ever hear from my Army buddies anymore.

And so that's when I told him what I hadn't even told Cindy, I guess because I'd never wanted to hear the words out loud. Now seemed the time to do it though.

I told him about how you went back for another tour, this time in Afghanistan, and how you and your boys got pinned down on that hill for most of two days, taking mortar fire and sniper fire the whole time, and how you all must have been huddling there listening nonstop for the sound of a drone or a jet or a missile or *anything*, but that when it finally came, everybody had already stopped listening.

I bet it took me fifteen minutes to tell him that story, what with me running out of breath right at the start, and having to stop talking again and again to keep from just losing it. The more I talked, the more the sunlight coming through the windshield stung my eyes. By the time I finished, my throat was thick and hoarse and my chest felt like it'd taken a direct hit from an RPG.

Afterward Pops was quiet for a while, and of course I was too. And then he started talking.

"When I came home from the A Shau, you know, I was so full of hate. Hated everybody, never trusted a thing I was told. Seeing your own gunships blowing your buddies to pieces all around you, and for what? For a useless chunk of land. That'll do something to a man. Plus the way the country was back then, that didn't help. Nobody ever said 'Thank you for your service' to us. Baby killer, that's what we got called. It was tough living with that every day. Tough living with what we did over there.

"Your grandmother, though, she waited it out with me. She kept right on loving me, you know, and waiting for things to heal. Then your mother came along, and it all kept getting better. Then you. My grandson. And I finally came to realize that nothing else really mattered. There wasn't nothing could touch the way I loved the three of you, and the way I knew you all loved me."

I felt like there wasn't anything I could say to that. Like he didn't want me to say anything. He only wanted me to listen.

"People don't have to be perfect for you to love them," he said. "You understand what I'm saying? Sometimes you love them because they aren't perfect. You love them for their imperfections . . .

"One thing you probably don't know is that I never entirely agreed with your grandmother's view of things. Church things primarily. I went to church with her, every Sunday, regular as clockwork. But I went because of her. What I mean is I went *for* her, not for myself or for any other reason."

I could see him struggling with it a little, not knowing exactly how to get to what he wanted.

"What is it you want to tell me, Pops?"

"Your grandmother would have told you, in fact she always did, that good can only come from good. You have to do good to be good."

"Sounds familiar."

"Well . . . she never went to war, did she?"

"Sir?"

"Good don't always beget good. And evil don't always beget evil. In fact sometimes it's the opposite that's true."

I kept driving, staring straight ahead, trying to keep my eyes clear.

"You did things over there you're not proud of," he said. "I know you did. I knew it the moment you came home and I looked into your eyes. It was like looking at myself in the mirror, that's how I knew. You don't have to tell me what it was, because that's not what's important. What's important is that you did what you had to do to get back home again. To get back from a place and a situation not one of us should ever have been sent to in the first place."

And I wanted to tell him, Spence. All the horrible things I saw and did and failed to do over there. I just couldn't get it out. All these years it's been stuck in my throat, half choking me. I guess maybe it always will be.

Pops didn't say anything for a long time after that. And all I could do was to keep driving with the road all blurry in front of me. After a while he put his arm up on the back of the seat, and he let his hand rest there on my shoulder. And that's where it stayed until we got to where we were going.

He had me pull off the side of a road out in the country. Off to the right was a cornfield, must have been a couple hundred acres or more. All the corn had been harvested and the stalks were mostly stubble now, short brown spears looking almost white in the sun.

"This is it," he said.

"We came out here for a cornfield?"

"Out there beyond it. See that hill with the one tree on top?"

"I do."

"Back when I was even younger than you, that hill out there was a dream of me and your grandmother's. I don't know how many picnics we had up there, but it was a lot. I'm pretty sure we made your mother up there one night."

He opened up the truck door and climbed out. I shut off the engine, then popped open my own door.

"I don't want you coming with me," he said. "In fact I don't even want you sitting down here watching me."

"Why not?" I asked.

"Because I want to be alone with your grandmother a little while. And that's the best place I can think to do it. I've been cooped up in that little apartment too long. The place is always noisy and filled with a bunch of busybodies won't give a man a moment's peace. And I miss her. I miss her every night. Are you going to begrudge me a little privacy while I spend a half hour or so with your grandmother?"

"No, sir. I'm not."

He stepped up closer and laid his hand on my shoulder. "Tell you what. About twenty miles back, on the far end of Main Street—the town's called Jamestown. You remember it?"

"Yes sir."

"There's this little store, red and white striped canopy out front. It's an old-time soda fountain. Your grandmother and I used to stop there sometimes. We'd get some hamburgers and a couple of root beers to go, and we'd bring them with us up to that hill."

"You think it's still open?" I said.

"We drove right past it not thirty minutes ago. Big red Open sign hanging in the window."

"What is it you want from there?"

"You go in and ask them for that old-fashioned root beer they sell. I can't think of the name of it now, but they'll know. See if you can get us a couple bottles."

"It will take me most of an hour probably."

"I've driven it plenty of times, son. I know how long it will take."

I looked toward the hill. "That hill's a good quarter mile away from here, Pops. I don't even see a path anywhere."

"You go through the corn. That's the only way to get there. But from up on top of that hill, you can see miles and miles all around. You can see a river, half a dozen little towns, mile after mile of trees and woods. Think how it must look on a day like this. I want to see it all again. Just me and your grandmother."

I didn't want to leave him, but I didn't want to disobey him either. I could see how important it was to him.

"Promise me that if you get tired . . ."

He looked back through the truck at me. "I'm not stupid, Rusty. Give me that much credit anyway."

"I've never once thought you were stupid, Pops."

He gave me a wink and a smile. Then he turned away and went into the field of stubble.

It took me twenty-five minutes to get back to Jamestown. I spent another fifteen driving up and down Main Street, looking for that red and white striped canopy. Finally I climbed out and asked a fellow not much younger than Pops where I could find the soda fountain. He pointed across the street to a Tru-Value Hardware store. I asked him how long the soda fountain had been closed down, and he said the early eighties. Eighty-three. Maybe eighty-four.

I sat there in the truck a couple minutes, trying to figure things out. Why had Pops lied to me? Or did he really believe the fountain was still there?

It didn't take me long to come to an understanding. I drove like a bat out of hell after that, even though I knew it wouldn't do me any good.

It wasn't until the next day, when I called Pops' doctor, that I found out about his heart. "Last time I saw him was three weeks ago," the doctor told me. "We found evidence of at least two previous infarctions, both fairly recent."

Knowing Pops, if the climb itself didn't do him in, he had plenty of time to go back down and up again, or to jog in circles around the top of that hill, whatever it took until he got what he went there to get. All I know for sure is that he was looking up into the sky when I found him. And he was grinning that grin of his, showing his beautiful white teeth, looking like he knew he'd put something over on me again.

*

I'm going to have to delete all this soon, Spence. I can't be keeping all this on my computer for somebody to find. I've known it a long time now but I really hate to do it. If you were here I bet you'd have an explanation for that feeling. I don't remember anything you couldn't eventually puzzle out.

The thing is, deleting this is going to feel like I'm the only one left anymore. I'm not saying that exactly right, I guess. What I mean is that all the people I counted on for advice from time to time will be gone forever now. First Mom. Then Gee. Then Pops. And now you.

And now I can almost hear you laughing at me. "Pull on your big boy pants and get to work," you're saying. "You keep sitting there with your creamy white ass hanging out, that big hairy elephant's going to sniff you out for sure."

So okay, I guess this is it. I just wanted you to know I've decided to keep paying rent on Pops' storage unit. Keep things the way they are for a while. I like to go there sometimes, just to sit in the darkness with the door closed, surrounded by those few things Pops and Gee and Mom cared about enough to keep, all those little pieces of the lives they lived and the ones I was lucky enough to share. That's where I am right now, in fact. Sitting here with my laptop on my knees. Trying to say another goodbye.

I just need to be by myself sometimes. Knowing now what I am, what I'm capable of, it's the best thing for me. So I'm lucky I have this place. This we'll defend, right? This we'll defend.

I especially like it here on cool fall days like this one, when the rain is beating down on the metal roof, and even a box of concrete and steel starts to smell like something fresh again, like maybe it really is halfway possible to box up the past and still enjoy it, still remember the good things and the good people, all the laughs and the love we shared together, without letting yourself be crushed flat by all the bad stuff behind it and all the bad stuff up ahead.

Despite everything that's happened, I still enjoy the rain. But I don't look at it anymore the way Gee did. She said it's God's way of washing everything clean and starting again. Me, I'm not so sure. I guess I believe we don't get anything like forgiveness in this lifetime, no matter how hard we pray for it. No matter where we hide the bad things we've done. Once done, they're always done. We can try to make something good out of it, which is what I intend to do with that drug money, though nothing for me. Not a penny of it for me. But even so, forgiveness is pretty much out of the question in the here and now. In this vale of tears, as Gee used to call it, all we get is the rain.

So I guess that's it. That's about all I've got to say. I won't be writing to you again, stirring up all the ashes of the past. It's time for me to put my shoulder to the wheel and concentrate on my little ones.

So long, my brother.

Spin and die . . .

And maybe, just maybe, who knows? Live again, butterfly.

ACKNOWLEDGMENTS

"The Caterpillar," by Christina Georgina Rossetti (1830–1894) is the source of Russell's lines about butterflies and caterpillars.

My thanks to my editors, Jessica Tribble and Charlotte Herscher, for their enthusiasm for and close attention to this novel. A book is only as good, or as wretched, as its editors. Over the course of my career, I have experienced both types. The wretched ones drag their heels, kick up the sod, and trail mud across every page, or else do nothing at all. The good ones tread lightly and tenderly through the writer's garden, pruning and replanting only when it heightens the reader's experience. Jessica and Charlotte occupy the latter group. My gratitude to both of you.

Few writers these days find prosperity in the literary thicket without an intrepid guide and champion, and mine is my agent, Sandy Lu. Without her machete-wielding skills opening the path for me, I would still be lost in the brambles, picking thorns from my flesh.

I am also deeply indebted to Lieutenant Colonel Troy C. Bucher of the US Army for his assistance with this novel. Now a Professor of Military Science at Oklahoma State University, LTC Bucher's more than twenty-six years of military service have included three deployments to Iraq, and three years of teaching at the NATO antiterrorism training center in Ankara, Turkey. Thank you, Troy, for not only correcting my use of outdated and inaccurate military terms but also for your many insights into the mind of a modern soldier. Your generosity of time and experience personify the code of selflessness and sacrifice that distinguishes the men and women who serve our country.

It has been my honor over the years to teach a few dozen young men and women who were current or former members of our military forces. I have read their stories and essays and poems, and many times sat with them as they quietly wept while recounting their experiences. And while I have often disagreed with the policies that send these extraordinary individuals off to war on foreign soil, and with the way they are treated when they return from those wars, my esteem for them is in no way diminished. Most of them leave their homes for service to this country with the noblest and purest of intentions; that they too often return to us with those intentions subverted and scarred only increases my respect for the beauty still intact deep in their hearts and souls. This book is dedicated to every one of them and their colleagues.

Although words and ideas from these individuals have found their way into this novel, the sentiments expressed are mine alone. Those sentiments were formed first as the son of a World War II Marine who, on duty in the South Pacific, never got to see his firstborn son, who passed away before our father could return home; then as a young man who, thanks to the luck of the draw, was awarded, to his relief and disappointment, a draft lottery number of 322 on December 1, 1969, when the jungles of Vietnam were in full flame; then as the friend or acquaintance of young men who came home from Vietnam forever changed, if they came home at all; then as an avid reader of Hemingway, James Jones, Mailer, O'Brien, and Caputo, all once young soldiers too; then as a father blessed with two cherished sons; and, finally, as a teacher of some of the bravest young men and women I have ever known. Thank you all, and God bless you all.

ABOUT THE AUTHOR

Randall Silvis is the internationally acclaimed author of more than a dozen novels, one story collection, and one book of narrative nonfiction. He is also a prize-winning playwright, a produced screenwriter, and a prolific essayist who has been published and produced in virtually every field and genre of creative writing. His numerous essays, articles, poems, and short stories have appeared in the Discovery Channel magazines, the *Writer*, *Prism International*, *Short Story International*, *Manoa*, and numerous other online and print magazines. His work has been translated into ten languages.

Silvis's many literary awards include two writing fellowships from the National Endowment for the Arts; the prestigious Drue Heinz Literature Prize; a Fulbright Senior Scholar research award; six fellowships for his fiction, drama, and screenwriting from the Pennsylvania Council on the Arts; and an honorary Doctor of Letters degree awarded for "distinguished literary achievement."